PU$$Y MAGNET

A Titans of Tech Novel

TESSA LAYNE

Paperback Edition ISBN-13: 978-1-948526-14-2
EPUB Edition ISBN-13: 978-1-948526-15-9
Published by Shady Layne Media

A Very Naughty RomCom

Let's get one thing straight. I love pussy. Fucking. Love. It.

Call me shallow, call me a perv, call me a fucking manwhore, but the reason I know there's a heaven is because God made pussy. Because when my tongue, fingers or cock is buried in its sweetness I know without a doubt, I'm in heaven.

My life's mission, to sample as much of the pussy garden as possible, began when I was thirteen and found a stack of playboy magazines in the shed out behind my grandfather's summer house. There, I was initiated into the exotic, mysterious world of pussy. Black pussy, white pussy, Asian pussy, Mexican pussy, Italian pussy, Irish pussy, Turkish pussy. Each a perfect pink flower, reflecting the personality of its owner - trimmed, waxed, or wild and free, they hold the key to a woman's undoing. Because no matter who a woman is, a ball buster in the courtroom or a flower child at an Avitt Brothers concert, I have the keys to the kingdom, and they all want it.

Until Mariah Sanchez - aka Sparky

She wants me.

I can feel it. I can *smell* it. But for nine months, sixteen days, twelve hours and forty-seven minutes she's had my cock in irons. Worse, my mouth and my fingers, too. Locked up in an invisible prison of my own making. And because I'm a stupid idiot, the only person I can blame for my predicament is me.

But that's about to change…

Chapter One

FROM THE PERSPECTIVE OF STEELE'S DICK

Football players are pussies. Baseball players? Pussies. Hockey players? Maybe not pussies, but with all the gear they hide under it's hard to tell.

You want to fuck a real athlete? Someone who's all muscle with endurance for days? The kind of athlete who can make you come for an hour straight? Then let me tell you where it's at. Crew.

What's that? You've never even heard of crew? Eight men in a boat, using one-hundred-percent of their God-given muscles, stressing every system in the body to the max in an all out sprint- just them against the water and the wind. Man against nature. You want a man with arms? With abs? With a rock hard ass? Oh- *and* a brain? Fuck the rest of the athletes. You want a man in a boat.

A man like… me.

Someone with a hot bod, an enormous cock, and a bank account with so many zeroes behind the number, it'll make your panties wet.

Chapter Two

"Dude, tuck your junk away." Sparky, my boat's coxswain, rolls her eyes as she walks past. "Press is on their way for a photo-op."

My chest puffs a little. "There's no tucking this bad boy away, Sparky. You know that. Especially when we smoked the competition."

She scoffs deep in her throat not bothering to turn around. "I'm putting you in the back row then. No one needs to see that shit on the front page of the London Times."

"Then they shouldn't design these uniforms so tight," chimes in my CTO and best friend Stockton Forde as he falls into step beside me.

"Right?" I add, following her down the dock to where the press and our fans wait to congratulate us. "The ladies don't give two fucks about rowing, or who wins a regatta. They're here for one thing only." I slide a glance Forde's direction.

"The uniforms." We both chortle simultaneously.

"Twelve-year-olds," Sparky mutters under her breath as she keeps walking.

I fucking love this about her. We all do. Being a female cox for an eight-man rowing team is half motivation, half toleration, and fulltime ego management. And Sparky has those qualities in spades. It's why we hired her fresh out of college to help whip our team back into shape. And today it's paid off big-time.

Sparky stops and turns on a dime, holding out her hands, and giving us one of those *I'm not fucking around* looks. "Don't be assholes in front of the press. No one likes losing at home." She looks all eight of us in the eye. "Steele, since you're stroke position, the press is going to be directing most of the questions to you."

This is why our team loves Sparky. She's so much more than a coxswain. She's the heart and soul of our boat, we do things with her we can't do on our own. And sure, Fitz, our official coach is a phenom when it comes to technique — to helping each of us understand timing, feathering the oar, and making our strokes as efficient and streamlined as possible. But it's Sparky that helps us make the boat swing. And when it swings like it did today, it's fucking magic.

"And the women," grumbles Owen, my CFO and the tallest guy on our boat. "Share the love with the other guys, asshole."

A ripple of laughter spreads through the group.

"There were three camped outside his hotel room this morning," adds Mac, our most powerful rower. Half Scot, half Italian, the guy is a beast.

"And two more inside," adds Jackson, our lawyer, cheerily throwing me under the bus.

I spread my hands. "Hey, I can't help it that the ladies love me." And I can't help it that I love the ladies. Their soft curves, the way they coo and purr when I lick their nipples into hard peaks. The way they arch and clutch the covers when I feast on their honeyed treasure. I refuse to collect wine because it would take more than a lifetime to sample all the good stuff. Same with pussy. Why limit myself to just one when there's a buffet of perfection waiting to be pleasured?

Sparky gives me the full-on evil-eye. "Just make sure they love you far from the cameras. We don't need any videos of your shenanigans posted online, got it?" She shakes her head and mutters something else under her breath that I don't quite catch.

My ears perk up. "What was that?"

Her eyes jerk back to mine, and I swear her sun-kissed cheeks darken a shade. "Don't forget to invite the London Rowing Club to a rematch at our regatta in August."

That's not what she said. I want to press the question, but now's not the time. Not with the reporters and the ladies practically crawling over the barriers. Instead I nod and follow as she turns and marches toward the meet and greet area where Fitz is already taking questions. She stops at a bench and motions for us to grab our sweats. "Gotta protect the family jewels," she says with a sly smile, pulling a pint-sized sweatshirt over her own head.

"Hey, what'd you say back there?" I ask.

"Let it go, Steele. It was nothing. Go meet your fans."

"They're your fans, too."

She glances over her shoulder at the throng of young co-eds clambering for a view from behind the wall of cameras. "I'm pretty sure they're not lesbians. Go let them down gently. And don't forget we have a three a.m. wake-up for the airport."

"Way to be a buzzkill, Sparks."

She flashes me a super-sized grin. "That's me, and you love it."

She's right about that.

Chapter Three

FROM THE PERSPECTIVE OF STEELE'S DICK

You can laugh all you want about cox in a box, or small cox winning big races, but let's get one thing straight… the size of your cox doesn't matter when you have the biggest dick.

Chapter Four

"What the fuck crawled up your ass and laid eggs?" Stockton asks when he sees I'm clutching my pint so hard my knuckles show white.

I nod across the pub. "You ever see Sparky like that?"

Stockton scans the room, eyes landing on Sparky. He bites back a grin. "You mean acting like a girl?"

"I mean talking to other boats," I growl.

Owen, my number six in the boat and four inches taller than me drops onto the bench next to me. "What's got your britches in a bunch? No ladies asking to feel your biceps?"

The pub is filled with older men and women my mother's age. And the team from Spain. No one here I'd be remotely interested in, which has given me time to watch Sparky. And more time to wonder what the fuck is up with her. Normally she sticks to us like glue, then bows out after a couple rounds. Tonight, she's been buying rounds… but not for us. We're the fucking winners and she's across the room buying rounds for the douchebag Spaniards. Seriously… What. The. Fuck?

Stockton leans across the table, talking to Owen in a stage whisper. "Sparky just broke up with her boyfriend."

I hold up a hand. "Wait, *what?*" I must be hearing things.

Owen covers a laugh. "What do you mean, *what*? Didn't you know? Sparky was practically married, and she threw the guy out last week."

I blink.

How in the fucking fuck did I not know this? I've been sitting directly across from Sparky for the better part of three years, pulling my ass off at her command. Letting her bootcamp my ass four times a week, and this is the first time I've ever heard about a boyfriend? Furthermore, why in Christ's nutcrackers am I the last person to find out? It's my fucking boat. I'm financing this goddamned gig. I should at least know what the fuck is going on with my cox. I slide a glance Sparky's direction. Her head is thrown back, throat undulating with a laugh that comes straight from her toes, short dark hair falling behind her like a puffball, and a smile so wide her face might split in two. She's laughed that hard with us, sure… but not like this. She looks… different.

Owen curses under his breath, and then louder. "Motherfucker. I know that look. Don't go getting any ideas, man."

"Seriously, man," Stockton adds. "You've got beer goggles. Owen's right. Do *not* go getting any ideas."

"I don't have any ideas, and I don't have beer goggles," I answer, not taking my eyes off Sparky, or the dudes on either side of her. Just then, the asshole to her left glances up and catches my eye. Then the corner of his mouth pulls up real slow as his chin lifts. As if he's already tapped her ass.

Over my dead body.

"We need to make an extraction," I growl.

"I think you're fucking psycho. Let Sparky have her fun. She can handle herself."

"Did you see the look that guy gave me?"

"You're paranoid," Owen says.

"I'm not. Shit's gonna go down if we don't step in."

"There a problem?" Mac steps up to join us.

I nod my head Spark's direction. "She's in trouble."

Mac takes a pull of his Guinness and surveys the scene unfolding across the room. "She looks like she's having fun." He side-eyes me with a smirk. "Sure this isn't about reminding the Spaniards your dick is bigger?"

It totally is, but my gut's screaming something's wrong. I drain what's left of my pint and rise. "I'm going in. Y'all join me if you're up for it." I let my midwestern, nearly southern twang come out. "Sparky's in trouble and we're not going to let her swing."

I'm halfway across the room before I register the groans of frustration and scraping benches behind me. My guys have my back, just like I'll have theirs- anytime they ask. I step up to the Spaniards' table, and drop my hand to Sparky's shoulder. She stops laughing and looks up. Our eyes lock and for a second my heart stops. Her eyes are bright, shiny, maybe even glassy — like she's had too much to drink. *Is she drunk?* Sparky can drink half the team under the table, and that's saying something, because our friend, Danny Pendergast, makes whiskey for a living. But it's the way her full lips are parted that makes my cock jump. A jolt of lust rips through me, like a power surge frying my circuits. It happens so fast that it's gone before it even registers, but what's left in its place is a bloodlust urge so strong I could be a fucking gladiator. "Time to go, Sparky," I growl, pulling my mouth back into a toothy smile I aim at the other guys.

"Whaddya mean, it's time to go?" she slurs. "Javi and I were just getting to know each other."

Motherfucker. She's three sheets to the wind. "*Cuanto le diste?*" I demand roughly, glaring at the other men?

"Wait…" She flails an arm. "You speak *Spanish?*"

The Spaniards look just as surprised. "Enough." I'm not great, but we have offices in Madrid, so I know enough to get by. Although I refuse to speak with a lisp. That shit's for pussies.

"*No lo se*," the guy she called Javi answers with a shrug, and a look that says, *don't ask me, man.*

"Time to go, Sparks."

She shakes her head, bottom lip thrusting out. "No."

"*No?*" I'm momentarily dumbfounded, that is, until my anger finds a voice. I lean close to her. "You're shithoused, and you're coming with me, sweetheart."

She beams at me. "You called me sweetheart." Her eyes slide down my torso and land on my cock. She cocks her head like she's studying my junk, then shakes it with a giggle. "You might have a perfect cock, but your charms won't work on me. I don't do —" Another giggle slips from her mouth. "*Pussy magnet*," she mumbles, half swallowing the words. But this time, there's no missing what she said.

Behind me, Owen and Mac guffaw.

She's wasted. There's no way sober Sparky would ever let shit like that fall from her lips. Heat flushes the back of my neck. I'm half mortified, half fluffed that she noticed my cock is perfect. "That's it," I grumble. "I'm taking you back to the hotel." I scoop her up into my arms, and she wraps an arm around my neck with a giggle, batting her eyelashes. I never noticed how thick and long her lashes were, or how her dark eyes are at least four different shades of brown, ranging from nearly black to almost gold. For a second I lose myself. Until she pokes a finger into my chest. "Pussy magnet, definitely," she says again, then circles her finger toward Stockton. "And *you*… I've heard your O's are legendary. And you two—" she swings her arm to Owen and Mac. "Big bad baby daddies."

"So we have... *nicknames?*" Stockton asks, incredulous.

"Are you fucking kidding me?" adds Owen with a shake of his head.

Mac puffs his chest with a grin. "Hell, yeah, my genes will make great babies."

"Of *course* you do. How do you think I keep track of you? Too much test'rone." she says with a hiccup. "Mr. Whiskey, Lady killer."

Damn if she hasn't named us all. "You're drunk and we're going to pretend this never happened," I say through gritted teeth, pushing through my friends and stalking to the door. "Right, guys?" I toss over my shoulder. Their 'yeahs' and 'sures' offer me little relief. There will be razzing. Maybe not in front of Sparky, but I know my teammates well enough to know I'm never going to live this down.

Chapter Five

FROM THE PERSPECTIVE OF STEELE'S DICK

Sparky's not wrong. On a cock scale of 1-10, I'm a fucking perfect. A 100, easy. I've been blessed with girth *and* length. But it's what I do with it that matters. I know just the angle to hit the mythic g-spot, and with my stamina built from years of rowing, I can go until my partners come at least twice. Minimum. And that's just from fucking.

But what makes me a pussy magnet, as Sparky so crassly, and without knowing it, perfectly put it — what keeps the ladies begging for more is my tongue. My tongue on their body, and most importantly, my tongue right where it matters most, their pussy. The key to a man's heart might be through his stomach, but the key to a woman's heart is definitely through her pussy. Ask any woman, straight up, they'll tell you a man's a keeper if he's a good guy, treats her right, *and* gives her regular head. A flick of the clit, a lap along her seam, a thrust into her honeyed opening, and they're dead in the most Shakespearean sense of the word.

And I fucking love it.

Chapter Six

We're not even halfway back to the hotel when she pukes all over both of us. "*Ohmygod*, I'm so sorry," she slurs, trying to wipe the contents of her stomach from my pants with a tissue she digs from her jeans.

"Let's just get you home," I say with a dark laugh, because seriously, this night could not be more of a clusterfuck. *Pussy Magnet? Baby Daddy?* I'm half-worried that Sparky's three quarters of the way to a nervous breakdown, and our season just started. Our boat's finally rocking, in large part, thanks to her, and visions run before my eyes of the fallout if she quits. I tip the Uber driver a hundred bucks for his trouble, and give him another two in cash.

"Oh, no." Sparky sways and shakes her head when I try to pick her up again. "I can walk b'mysel."

I keep my hand firmly at the top of her arm. "Whatever you say, sweetheart." There's no way she could find the elevator in her state, let alone her room. "Give me your room key."

She blinks.

"Your key. Tell me you have your key…Sparky?" I add after a pause. Her face says it all. She's going to puke again. I tug on her arm. "Over here sweetheart. Try and aim for the bushes."

She lets fly again, heaving out the contents of her stomach. I'm stunned there's anything left after the way she puked all over the back seat of the car. Sparky turns to me, eyes wide. Fuck, she's going to cry. "Oh no, sweetheart," I say, making an executive decision. "You're *not* going to cry. Everything's okay. Everyone pukes at least once in their lives." I flash her a reassuring smile. "C'mon. Upstairs we go." I hustle her to the elevator, praying no one steps in with us. We reek.

She catches my eye in the gilded mirror and cocks her head. "In another time, another place, Steele."

"What's that supposed to mean?" Seriously. What. The. Fuck? She gives me an amused smile, and lifts a shoulder, clutching the railing as she sways right into my chest. "That's it," I grunt, sweeping her into my arms again. "You're in no condition to walk." I burst out of the elevator, ignoring her protests and hurry down the hall, around the corner, and down another long corridor to the suite at the end. I extract my room key and get her inside, making a beeline for the bathroom. "We're cleaning you up." I desperately need cleaning too, but I can wait. "Can you stand while I help you out of your clothes?"

"Are we getting naked?" She grins.

"I swear I'm not going to look. You can shower in your underwear if you want, but we're covered in puke."

"We're getting naked," she singsongs. Her hand comes to the buttons on her shirt. "Promise you won't look?"

"That would just be weird."

"Why?" A flirty smile teases the corner of her mouth.

I pause. Until tonight, I've never thought of Sparky as anything other than Sparky, and I'm pretty sure the guys would saw off my balls with a rusty knife if I made a pass at her. Hell, I'd do the same to any of them. But the thought of doing something with Sparky wakes my dick up in a big way. Not. Good. I sigh heavily. "Because you're my cox."

"So?" she challenges, fingers popping the first button. I catch a hint of paler flesh.

"And the guys would kick my ass if we did anything," I finish, knowing the answer is a cop-out. Reluctantly, I turn around, fighting the dirty thoughts that pop into my head. I've seen Sparky in a uniform, her tits aren't big, but I can't help wondering what they'd feel like against my palm. My cock agrees wholeheartedly. Worse, I'm suddenly dying to see her pussy. Because holy hell, she's a firecracker in the boat, a total ass-kicker. Is she that fierce in bed? Or does she surrender, all soft and compliant?

Her shirt lands on the floor. "Who says they'd have to know?"

I bite back a groan. "Fuck, Sparks, you're wasted. I'd never take advantage of you like this."

"Even if you liked me?"

I hear her stagger and turn just in time to catch her before she pitches into the sink. "*Especially* if I liked you," I say through gritted teeth, forcing my eyes to the floor and away from the pink lace bra that flashes in the corner of my eye. "Now, sit down while I help you."

I drop to the floor and remove her high-heeled boots. I think this is the first time I've seen her wearing something other than athletic shoes. I'm even more surprised by the pink toenail polish. "When did you paint your nails?"

"I *always* paint my nails on race day," she says with a giggle.

"You're kidding."

"Just because I'm in a boat with too much testosterone," she slurs the word, "doesn't mean I can't be girly."

"You can be as girly as you want sweetheart," I answer wryly. "Stand up, so I can help you out of your pants." She stands, clutching my hair for balance while I fiddle with the buttons on her jeans, averting my eyes when I yank them down her legs. I bite back another groan when I catch a glimpse of matching panties covering a thatch of dark curls. As soon as her pants are off, I sit her back down and turn on the water. "Do you think you can stand on your own?"

"Nope," she answers cheerily.

I let out a string of curses as I strip to my boxer briefs, glad to at least be rid of my puke-ridden clothing. "Okay, let's get you into the shower." She reaches around her back to remove her bra. "Why don't you leave that on?"

Her eyes scan up my chest, and in spite of her drunken state, there's no missing the hunger there. "I don't shower with my clothes on," she says primly, as if I've asked her the opposite.

"You never make anything easy, do you?" I mutter under my breath as I help her up, looking everywhere but at her. My cock is straining against my shorts, but there's no way I'm removing them. Someone has to keep their head on straight.

She gasps. "Is *that* because of me?" She pulls a finger up the ridge of my cock.

I freeze. And then I look. Her face is unguarded, perfectly fascinated, as if she were examining a wildflower and not my most precious appendage. Her tits are high and perky, soft round globes punctuated with taut nipples the most beautiful shade of dusky brown. In spite of the fact that Sparky's as ripped as any of us, there's still a gentle curve to her belly leading down to an untamed garden of dark curls. I love it. So. Fucking. Much. And the thought of what she looks like when she comes, tortures me.

A slow grin curves her mouth. "So *this* is why they call you the Man of Steel."

I hate that nickname, even if it's true. "It's what I do with it," I snap back. *And my mouth and my fingers.*

She strokes it again, as if she needs to gather more information. "Definitely a pussy magnet," she mumbles under her breath, swaying into me.

I grab her hand, even while my dick is yelling at me to let her keep going. "Mariah... *please.*" My voice comes out strangled. I'm not above begging right now. Somehow, by some miracle, I manage to get her into the hot water without feeling her up. All I can say is I better get an extra cushy spot in heaven for this, because Mariah Sanchez is temptation in the flesh. "Brace your hands against the wall," I say roughly, wishing I was saying that for purposes other than cleaning her up. I think of my mother, my grandmother, Antarctica, hairy men. Anything to keep my raging boner in check. I squirt a dollop of shampoo into my palm, and work it into her short, dark hair. She moans and leans into my fingers. "Shut your eyes," I say, refusing to watch the suds cascade down her spine. My imagination is doing well enough on its own without the added visual. I pull conditioner through, then soap up a washcloth. I scrub as quickly as I can, ignoring her little mewls and shoulder rolls. I scrub until her tawny skin is pink.

"You missed a spot."

I know exactly what I missed. "You'll be fine," I say briskly.

"But-"

"No buts," I interrupt, while I quickly scrub down. I hate this. Platonic showers suck. And right now, I just want to get this torture over with and forget it ever happened. I tilt the spray my direction, not trusting Sparky to remain upright if I ask her to move. As soon as the water's off, I pick her up, ignoring the way her breasts press against my chest, and step out of the tub.

She loops her hands around my neck. "Mmmm, nice."

Too nice. Way too fucking nice, and damn me to the seventh circle of Hell, I'll be replaying that scene over and over in my mind, wishing the outcome had been different. I set her on her feet and grab the terry cloth robe hanging on the back of the door. "Here."

She holds out one arm, and then the other, and I close the robe, tying it securely around her tiny waist. An ache springs to life in my chest, an unfamiliar longing. She looks so small and vulnerable engulfed in a robe that sits comfortably on my six-foot-three-inch frame.

"Damn you, Sparky," I mutter, turning around to drop my soaking boxer briefs. My cock springs free, still hard as a spike. I wrap a towel around my waist, then pick her up and stride to the bed. She's wasted enough, I'm worried she'll pass out. Or worse, choking if she pukes in her sleep.

Her eyes soften as she stares up at me once I've settled her against my chest. "I always did like you, Steele."

Again, an unfamiliar longing comes over me. "Go to sleep, Sparks," I murmur, pushing an unruly lock from her forehead and dropping a kiss in its place, and inhaling the scent of her mixed with cheap shampoo. It will be the only kiss we ever share. It has to be. Even though my dick wants to throat punch me now for making that call. I doze off, replaying images of Sparky in various states of dress.

Chapter Seven

FROM THE PERSPECTIVE OF STEELE'S DICK

I still have vivid memories of finding my grandpa's stash of playboys in the garage the summer I was thirteen. I can't remember why I was in the garage in the first place, but I'll never forget the first centerfold I looked at. A dark-eyed brunette stared out at me, with parted lips and a half smile, titties full and a little droopy with dark areolas and pink nipples. She pinched one, but I couldn't look away from her other hand — the way it teased open her pussy, shaved except for a strip of neatly trimmed fur in the shape of a heart. It was pink, and plump, and it gave me an instant boner. My mouth watered. I just stared and stared. Until I heard my grandpa hollering and I scrambled to hide the evidence of my snooping.

I snuck out to the garage every day that summer, picking a different magazine each time. By the end of the summer I was in love with women.

Chapter Eight

Sparky jerks awake with a groan, which yanks me from a deliciously dirty dream. I'm not ready to let go of either. "My head," she says tightly, face wrinkling in pain. But then her eyes fly open and she scrambles away with a horrified gasp. "*Ohmygodwhatdidwedo?*" Her pitch rises to an ungodly frequency as she gives me the stink-eye, followed by another groan as she pinches her temples. "Tell me please we didn't..." her voice sounds panicked.

I can't help but laugh. This is the Sparky I know and love. Still, I can't resist having a little fun with her. "Would it be so bad if we did?"

"Eww. Awful."

"That's not what you said last night," I retort, stung.

She pulls open the robe far enough to look down. "Oh god, I'm—"

"Naked," I supply. "As the day you were born."

"You didn't," she says, clearly scandalized.

"Nope, but you did." The corner of my mouth pulls up.

The color drains from her face and she buries her head in her hands. "What exactly did I do?"

"Don't worry, you'd remember if we did. I'd make sure of it," I can't resist adding.

She snorts, shaking her head. "So cocky."

I open my hands in surrender. "It's hard not to be when even you can't keep your hands off of me."

Her head snaps up and she pins me with a glare. "I have standards, Steele."

It's my turn to snort. "And I believe I surpassed them all last night."

"You're bullshitting me," she accuses.

Okay, maybe I am, just a little. But I'm irritated as fuck that she's horrified at the thought of having sex with me. "You called me a man of steel, among other things."

"What else did I say?" she asks faintly.

"Things only a lover would say." I bite the inside of my cheek to keep from laughing. "But it's okay. I fended you off and your dignity remains intact."

She scoffs. "As if. I'd never, not in a million years, rock the boat with you."

"Why the fuck not?"

She gives me a look that can only say *fucking duh.* "For starters, you're my stroke."

"Yes I am." I grin.

"Get your mind out of the gutter, Steele," she scolds, and continues. "Second. You don't know me."

"Like hell, I don't."

She gives me *that* look again. "Really?"

My stomach sinks. It eats at me that she's right. "I know you," I protest.

"What's my favorite song?"

Damn. I give her my winningest smile.

"See? What about my favorite food?"

"Pizza?"

She shakes her head.

"Fish and chips? I saw you eat fish and chips last night."

"We *all* ate fish and chips last night."

I madly reach into my memory for any clue of what she likes based on our past team hangouts. I come up with a big fat zero. But I'm determined not to let her win. "Ah-*ha,*" I cry, pointing my finger to the ceiling. "You paint your toenails every race day."

Her eyes go wide.

"See?" I press. "Besides, I would get to know you."

"You're so full of shit," she says with a laugh. "You don't get to know anyone. Not women, at least. They pass through your bed like water through a sieve. You can barely remember their names, let alone important details like when their birthday is, or what's their favorite flower."

I open my mouth to object, but she's right. The only attention I've paid to the women I've been with has been to mark their breathing, or the heat of their skin under my hands, or the way their legs tighten around my shoulders just before they come. "I pay attention to the things that matter."

"Like what? A woman's cup size?" Her mockery stings. And just like her brutal morning workouts, she doesn't let up. "I don't think you know the first thing about dating. About *wooing.*"

"*Wooing?* Who the fuck woos?" I ask incredulously.

"Normal men. Men who want to date and settle down."

"Well I don't want to settle down." Why would I? "Women are like wine. It's going to take a lifetime to experience them all."

She lets out a horrified gasp. "Did you seriously just compare me to a bottle of wine?"

"Not you specifically. But you know what I mean - why would I settle for just one woman?"

"Because you're incapable of maintaining even the most basic of relationships. You might be a machine in the boat with a hot bod and damn near perfect junk, but you only think of where your next lay is coming from."

"That is *not* true," I protest. "I always think about making things enjoyable — *beyond enjoyable* — for my partner. That's my top priority."

"Orgasms are your priority," she states flatly.

"Sure. Isn't that the point?"

She makes that scoffing noise in the back of her throat again. "No, actually it's not. Orgasms are nice — don't get me wrong — but I don't need a relationship for that. What about companionship? Friendship? *Intimacy?*" She skewers me with another withering glance, but I'm fixated on her implied admission that she masturbates. My mind instantly goes to the dirty place. "See?" she presses. "You can't even look at me. You can't have a real conversation with someone you've known three years. You have no idea who I am."

Now I'm pissed. I'm so frustrated I want to throttle her. Or kiss her silly. I lean forward. "I know enough. I know that your face flushes when you think you've been caught saying something naughty. I know that your breasts could fit perfectly in the palm of my hand. I know the exact look in your eye when you're thinking filthy thoughts, and I know *for certain* that you've never had a mind-blowing orgasm. One that shatters you completely."

Her mouth drops open, partly from shock, but I also see a flash of heat in her eyes.

I press my advantage. "I may not know what your favorite ice-cream is, or how you got the scar above your left eyebrow, but I know how to make you pant until you think you're going to die from the wanting, and I sure as hell know how to make you shout my name. And while we're at it—*you* don't know *me* either. So who's the bigger asshole?"

She rolls her lips together, and for a split second I think she might close the distance between us and kiss me. But it passes as she grins like I just made a deal with the devil. "I think I just made my point."

I cross my arms. "And what is that?"

She arches a brow. "I'd bet all the money in my bank account that you can't go without sex in the name of getting to know someone. Or letting someone get to know you."

"Like hell I can't," I growl, chest growing tight at her accusation.

The corner of her mouth curls up. "Yeah? Prove it."

"I will go without sex as long as it takes wipe that superior looking expression off your face."

My insult misses the mark, because she snickers and grins broadly. "One. Year."

Motherfucker.

I swallow and keep my face carefully neutral. I haven't gone without sex for more than a few weeks since I lost my virginity to Lara Niedermeyer when I was seventeen.

"Still think you can do it?" she taunts.

I'll be damned if I let Sparky get the better of me. "Fuck, yes. In fact, if I can't, I'll quadruple the money in your bank account. Hell, I'll make it a million." How hard can it be, really? I have enough zeroes in my bank account that I won't miss a mil, not that I plan on letting her best me.

"That's big talk from a guy with your reputation."

"And what exactly is my reputation? What did you call me last night? A *pussy magnet?*"

Her cheeks flush deep red. "Well, you are," she mutters, dropping her eyes.

I lean forward. So close I can smell last night's soap on

her skin. "And with good reason," I say, voice dropping to seductive levels as a very wicked thought enters my head. "And when I win this stupid wager, you're going to give me something in return."

"And what is that?" she asks a little breathlessly.

"One. Night."

Chapter Nine

FROM THE TEXTS OF MARIAH SANCHEZ AND HER SISTER

Mariah: Sooo… I think I made a pass at Steele last night…
Cecilia: WHAT?!?!?!?
Mariah: shrug emoji, facepalm emoji, crazy face emoji
Cecilia: Are you fucking kidding me?
Mariah: grimacing emoji
Cecilia: wtf happened? I WANT TEA
Mariah: I started drinking with the Spanish team…
Mariah: … And it's fuzzy after that. Except I woke up in Harrison's arms, wearing nothing but his robe.
Cecilia: O_O
Cecilia: Did you finally do the deed with the Man of Steel??!?!?
Mariah: I don't think so…
Cecilia: You don't think so?!? That was a y/n question.
Mariah: I know… but I don't remember. grimace emoji, facepalm emoji, head exploding emoji
Cecilia: Jesus.
Mariah: Don't let mom catch you swearing in text form.
Cecilia: I'll fucking swear if I want to.
Mariah: lol

Cecilia: you're distracting
Mariah: ya think?
Cecilia: Why? What else is there?
Mariah: Well aside from the fact that I'm pretty sure I puked over both of us, I got into an argument with his hotness.
Cecilia: OH? Chin on hands…
Mariah: It's too much to go over in text form, and we're just about to board the plane, but I might have goaded him into staying celibate for a year….
Mariah: And then he goaded me into agreeing to a one-night stand if he does it.
Cecilia: ARE YOU OUT OF YOUR FUCKING MIND?!?!?!?!?
Mariah: Apparently. But there's no way he'll last a whole year. This is Harrison we're talking about.
Cecilia: DETAILS. I WANT DETAILS.
Mariah: Can't. They just called our section. I'll call when I get home. Luv U - kissing emoji, heart eyes emoji.

From the perspective of Steele's dick

ay 10 of enforced celibacy

What. The. Fuck?

Seriously.

What the fuck kind of game is the dumbass upstairs playing? I have needs, man.

Chapter Ten

FROM THE PERSPECTIVE OF STEELE'S DICK

***ay 22 of enforced celibacy***

I hate him. Fucking *hate* him.

The redhead at the bar? Total prospect. And she's staring at us.

She's coming over, but he fucking cuts me off. Who the fuck thinks of hairy backs and armpit hair when there's a beautiful woman making a pass at us? Jesus fucktits.

Noooooo.

I'll be in my bunk.

Chapter Eleven

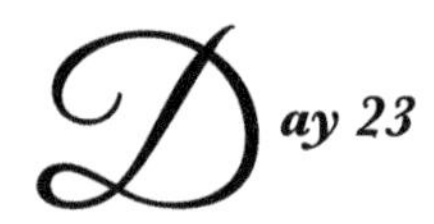***ay 23***

Sparky catches my eye and smirks as she settles herself on the cox box. "Rough night last night?"

I grunt and check my grip. She knows *exactly* how rough it was.

She chuckles quietly. "I think you need to up your workouts. Add more bicep curls?"

I glare at her.

She tsks and shakes her head, adjusting her headset. "Nothing stopping you from getting laid, Steele."

Except our fucking wager.

She turns on the mic. "Let's go. An easy five-hundred to warm up." Her eyes sparkle as they meet mine. "Ready, stroke?"

I pull too hard, eliciting grumbles from the stern.

"Easy there, Tex," Sparky chastises. I exhale roughly and force my roiling emotions to the bottom of the boat. "On my count. Ten… nine… eight…"

I let the sound of her voice lull me into the mental space where I become a pulling machine, blunting the razor sharp edges of my anger, and narrowing my focus to the rhythm of breath, push with the legs, lean back, pull with the arms, lift, feather, reach, repeat. There's a mind-numbing comfort in the repetition, the familiar ache that enters my muscles as we glide to the middle of the lake.

"Way enough," Sparky calls. "Let's review the race plan."

Tomorrow afternoon, we fly to Oregon for another race. We know the score. We've done this hundreds of times, and it's part of what makes Sparky great at what she does. Quiet descends on us as we shut our eyes and concentrate on the story Sparky weaves.

"Two warm-up laps, taking it nice and easy, until we line up in lucky lane three with the covered bridge at my back."

I don't know why we like lane three, but we do. And we always seem to pull better in that position. Some teams like the outside, we like the middle.

"There's only a light breeze, and there's just enough cloud cover, we lose the glare on the water. The starting gun fires, and we pull away, a nice slow twenty-five."

This is the same tactic we employed in London, a slow start, picking up the pace every hundred meters until we're five-hundred from the end, and then an all out sprint. Sparky leads us through every transition in perfect detail, down to the level of chop on the water. I shut my eyes, trying to stay focused on her words, but my thoughts keep drifting back to her mouth, and the way it twitches at the corner when she's amused, like she's trying not to smile.

"Steele? *Steele,*" she hisses, fingers covering her mic. "Are you ready?"

"Of course," I answer, wondering what the hell I missed while my mind was wandering.

"Did you even hear what I said?"

"Of *course.*"

Stockton snickers behind me. "*Bullshit,*" he coughs, then clears his throat. "She asked when was the last time you'd been given a BJ."

My eyes snap to Sparky. Her mouth twitches in a way that says she knows *exactly* when the last time I had any anything. But it *does* give me an idea. She didn't say anything about fooling around. Only sex. My dick gives a fist pump. Hell, yeah. I'm getting something tonight, even if it's not sex. My mood lightens considerably. In fact, when I leave the office with Stockton and Owen and head over to Danny's Whiskey Den, there's a spring in my step and I'm fully on the prowl…

Until prospect number one leaves me cold.

Stockton cocks his head. "You feeling all right, man? You haven't been yourself lately."

I'm not about to explain why. I shrug it off and signal for another round. "Any more headway made on where you think the cyber attacks are coming from?"

"Penny's on it, and I'm heading back to help her before I go home to pack," Stockton answers, raising a skeptical eyebrow. My answer didn't fool him in the least. But I'm at least grateful that he and his assistant Penny-the-Wonder-Hacker are on it. This is the third time we've been hit this month. Whoever they are, they're trying to probe our vulnerabilities, and I aim to stay six steps ahead of them.

Owen, my CFO, isn't as easily dissuaded, and after Stockton takes his leave, he turns to me. "I've never seen you turn down a woman, and in the last month I've seen you turn down, what…" he counts on his fingers. "Ten?"

I flash him a tight smile. "I'm taking a break. That's all."

"What in the hell for?"

"Why in the hell not?"

"Because you're… well, *you.*"

I get his implication. As a team, we've agreed to never speak of *the night.* Sparky would die if she knew how out of hand she'd been that night in London, and we don't want to risk the havoc it would create in the boat by losing her. She's one of a kind. I lose myself in the memory of her voice earlier today. It's always on the husky side from yelling at us. But something hooked deep inside me this afternoon as she was calling strokes. I pulled for her, just like I always do. But this time I had to shut my eyes, because all I could see was her pushed up against a wall, legs wrapped around me as she called stroke into my ear while I filled her with my cock. When I opened my eyes, her eyes were locked on me like a laser beam. I swear I saw the electricity jump between us, and there's no way I can tell that to Stockton or Owen, or anyone else in the boat. They'd skin me alive.

For a split second, I consider going to confession. But then prospect number two sits down next to us. Owen flirts with her briefly, but it's clear I'm the one she's after. She's a stunner. Long black hair cascading down her back, wide hazel eyes, and the legs of a dancer. Legs that at any other time, I would take back to my apartment and wrap around my neck. But something's definitely wrong with my Johnson because she leaves me cold.

Owen arches a brow and throws me a lifeline. "We'd love to stay and chat, but duty calls," he rises with an easy grin. "Catch you another time?"

It's not until we're halfway back to the office that he stops in the middle of the sidewalk. "You're full of shit if you tell me this isn't about a woman."

I open my hands. "To be honest, I don't know what it is."

And then it hits me like the streetcar flattening a penny. I want Sparky.

Chapter Twelve

I'm not at all happy about this development. In fact, as soon as I get home, I put on my running shoes and sprint a 10k. It does nothing to erase the taste of desire from my mouth. To make matters worse, my splits are so fast, that I want to call Sparky. I'd never call the guys to brag about a split time, but Sparky totally gets why it's a big deal. The faster I run, the faster the entire boat pulls. I'm the human fucking metronome. If I drive the pace, they'll follow. I'm so pumped, I want to hit the gym, even though it's well past ten. The secret to rowing is both insane cardio and forcing your lactic acid laden muscles to perform, even when they have nothing left.

I pace the lobby of my penthouse for a full minute before I abandon the idea of the gym. We're supposed to rest so we're fresh for Saturday's Covered Bridge race in Oregon, but I have too much energy. I circle my apartment like a caged lion, thumb twitching. After a beer and three more circles through my empty rooms, I give in.

I text Sparky.

HS: Hey…
Not the best opener I could have come up with, but it's late, and clearly I'm out of my mind.

MS: …
MS:
MS: …
MS:

"Fucking say something already," I mutter, watching the dots appear and disappear.

MS: Is everything okay?

"No. Everything is not okay," I bite. Figures she would ask that. I've never texted her for any reason other than to confirm workouts and practices. But how in the hell am I supposed to tell her that? My thumbs spell out a quick reply.

HS: Yup. Fine.

This is awkward as fuck. Before I can stop myself, I ring her.

"Are you *sure* everything's okay?" her husky voice sends a ripple of arousal down my spine.

I clear my throat. "Yeah. Yeah. I ran a thirty-four 10k." I can't help the smile that spreads my mouth, or the pride that creeps into my voice.

"Just now? At ten-forty-two when you're supposed to be sleeping?"

"You're not sleeping."

"I'm also not running. And the only thing I need to rest is my voice."

"I'd hate for it to lose that sexy scratch," I blurt before I can censor myself. I catch a quick intake of breath before the silence stretches between us. Fuuuuuuck. I should have stuck to texting. "I'm sorry, I shouldn't have said that." My gut clenches in the silence. I'm a fucking idiot. Reason number 678 why I don't do relationships.

Then she laughs. A throaty, rich sound that sends ripples of awareness shooting through my midsection. "Have you been drinking?"

I scoff. "No."

"Then it must be your dick talking." Her voice turns sympathetic. "Are you having trouble being celibate?" she teases with a giggle.

Of *course* I am. My balls are so blue they're violet. But I'd die before I admit that to Sparky.

"You can give it up, you know."

"So I can lose a cool mil? I don't think so."

She laughs again, more softly this time. "It'd be the easiest mil I ever made."

"I bet. And what would you do with said mil?"

"I'd go back to school and get my PhD."

I'm surprised by her answer. For starters, she answers so quickly, I know it's something she's thought about. A lot. I've never once considered Sparky might be interested in academics. It never occurred to me to ask. She's always been a female jock we work out with, row with, and drink with. I don't like the tight feeling that spreads across my chest. What I know about the guys in the boat could fill a library. That's just the way it is. The boat works because our trust runs deeper than professional respect. They're my brothers. But what I know about Sparky could fill a thimble. Guilt nags at me. Obviously she's confided in some of the other guys, *but not me.* That nags at me too. "PhD, huh? What would you study?" I keep my voice light.

"Sixteenth-century Spanish literature."

"Whoa. Is that even a thing?"

"Of course it is," she answers sharply.

"Sorry," I rush. "I was just surprised, that's all."

"Oh it's fine." I hear the disappointment in her voice. "I know it's not very practical. It's just something I love," she finishes softly.

"Then you should do it."

"Yeah. Maybe someday." Her tone of voice says loud and clear she thinks someday will never come.

"Why not now?"

"Because not all of us have bank accounts with gazillions of zeroes at the end," she scoffs. "I need to eat. And I love being in the boat," she adds after a pause.

"Ahh, so you can't serve two mistresses." I get that. I missed my shot at the Olympics by inches. And while I still dream about what might have been, I love making millions more. Nothing compares to the rush of closing a deal, not even an Olympic medal.

"There's no age limit on knowledge. I'll go back to school when I retire."

I hate that she puts it that way, but I know what she means. "But that's a long way off."

"It is," she agrees slowly. "But what's not a long way off is our flight tomorrow." She yawns into the phone. "Go to sleep, Steele."

"Did you just fake a yawn to get me off the phone?" I'm sixty-eight-percent sure she did.

Her breathy laugh sends ripples down my spine. "Maybe."

My dick snaps to attention. "You wouldn't fake

anything else, would you?" I can't help but ask, because again, a picture of her in the throes of ecstasy hovers at the edge of my mind.

She snorts. "That's for me to know and for you never to find out. But for the record," she continues after an awkward silence. "I never fake anything."

I go to sleep with the picture of her face firmly entrenched in my mind.

Chapter Thirteen

FROM THE PERSPECTIVE OF STEELE'S DICK

Let me tell you why rowers make the best lovers. Sta-mi-na. Rowers don't flame out. We're used to stroking with burning lungs, using every aching muscle in our body to propel the boat forward. Sex is a cakewalk. You want it hard and fast? I'm your man. You want it slow and sweet? I'll rock you all night long.

Chapter Fourteen

"On my count," Owen calls, swinging Sparky's ankles. "One, two, *three.*" We let go and Sparky flies into the water with a squeal. I remain on the deck while Owen, Stockton, and Mac follow her in. It's tradition to dunk the cox after a win, and normally I'd be right there in the water with the rest of my teammates, but something's subtly shifted between me and Sparky, and now our glances are loaded with something else. Something more than the general camaraderie we've enjoyed until now. I'm afraid if I touch her, I'll be found out. One of the guys is sure to notice. In fact, from the way Stockton eyes me, I'm sure he's noticed. I look away, hoping like fuck he won't bring this up later when we have celebratory beers.

"Here," I say gruffly, handing Sparky a towel and demanding my dick stand down when I glimpse her nipples pushing against her wet uni.

"Thanks." Her voice is hoarse from shouting. It tickles my insides like fingernails raking across heated skin. And when our hands collide as she takes the towel, I hear her sharp gasp. The sound shoots straight to my groin, pulling everything tight. "Great race today." Her eyes sparkle. "We can check with Fitz, but I'm pretty sure that last five-hundred was our fastest split ever."

"Damn straight it was," interjects Mac. "You took off like a bat out of hell when Sparky called for ten big ones. What the fuck happened?"

"Right?" adds Mac, wrapping a towel around his waist. "I could barely keep up."

How do I tell them I was working to get away? That the heat in Sparky's eyes when she called for ten big ones, pulled my balls tight with a breath stealing ache. I couldn't look away. Her eyes trapped me, burned through me, saw into the dirtiest, filthiest part of my soul. So I did something I've never done before, and should never do again. I didn't pull for the team. I didn't push with my legs and dig deep for myself either, not for some kind of a lofty purpose or a higher calling. I rowed for something much baser - I pulled for *her.* I burned out my quads and my glutes and laid back with everything I had, for every fantasy involving Sparky that's kept me from sleep, I pulled with laser focus praying that exhaustion would take over and smother the flame burning inside me.

It didn't.

It was the most exhilarating race I've been in since our team lost by inches at the Olympic trials. But unlike last time, I'll be marking this occasion with a cold shower and a handful of ibuprofen instead of an all-night romp with a couple of co-eds.

Adulting fucking sucks.

I turn away with a noncommittal grunt before I let the cat out of the bag and ruin everything. But I can't get away. Sparky follows me down the dock. Her hand is gentle, even tentative, on my arm. "Are you okay?"

"Fine," I grit. "Tired." I refuse to look at her, part of me terrified of what I might find in her face.

"Back there," she starts. "In the boat."

"It was nothing. You did a great job. I haven't performed like that since college," I add sincerely. The last thing I want is weirdness between us.

It's even worse later on at the bar. Everyone claps me on the back like I'm some kind of a fucking hero, when really, I'm just a dirty bastard hot for my cox. But we all know how crewmance kills a boat, so unless I quit, or sack Sparky, I'm dead in the water with no blades, no rudder, and no way to get out of my predicament.

"Hey, Steele, have you met Mandy?" Sparky calls, her hand on my arm again.

I turn, coming face to face with one of the women from the local rowing club. She's got to be at least six feet, and built. Female rowers are all Amazons, most of them over six feet and as lean as any of my guys. But Mandy has been blessed with height and curves, and from the look on her face, a healthy interest in my dick.

My dick should be singing… *schwinging…* doing a goddamned happy dance. But there is something seriously wrong with me, because… nothing. Nada. Not even a twitch. Until I make eye-contact with Sparky, who's smirking at me like she's pulled the biggest joke. *That's* hot. The way the corner of her mouth pulls in and her full lips twitch because she's trying oh, so hard not to burst out laughing.

She clears her throat. "I think you and Mandy have a lot in common."

"Do we," I state dryly. I can't wait to hear how.

Sparky's eyebrows lift, eyes widening. "Yeah. She owns a tech company."

"Oh? Tell me more." So Mandy has brains. Not surprising. Rowing isn't for the faint of heart. You have to be a bit psycho to torture your body the way we do, and that attracts risk takers - entrepreneurs, hedge fund managers, and people who climb Everest for shits and grins. I've never met a female rower who wasn't a ball-buster at least on some level. And while I've never fucked another rower, I have to admit the prospect is tempting. Except that Mandy isn't who I'd choose. My gaze flicks to Sparky, who wears an almost triumphant expression.

And the pieces fall into place.

I extend my hand, interrupting her elevator speech. "Real nice to meet you Mandy. The next time you're in Kansas City, drop by our offices. Remind my secretary where we met." It's a fucking platitude, but if she has the stones to do it, I'll remember. I never forget a face. "But you'll have to excuse me, my cox owes me a shot."

Sparky's eyes widen.

It's probably the competitor in me, but I fucking love turning the tables. "You owe me for the pain I'm going to be in tomorrow." I take Sparky's elbow and hustle her to the patio and the outside bar that backs up to a pond with a little fountain in the middle and too many geese. My teammates are playing darts with the women from Mandy's boat, and drinking out of the trophy. Given that I drained the trophy not ten minutes ago, it's unlikely they'll miss me anytime soon. I signal the bartender. "Two Patrón."

"Since when did you start drinking Patrón?"

I narrow my eyes. "Since last Cinco de Mayo when you started doing body shots off the Boston Rowing Club guys."

"You noticed that?"

I lean in. "I noticed a whole helluva lot more than that, Sparks."

Her eyes flash with the heat I've become all too familiar with, and she rolls her lips together, covering a smile. "Yeah?" She leans in too. Close enough, I catch a whiff of spicy citrus perfume. "What else?"

I hesitate, torn between wanting to lay my cards on the

table and the security of keeping them close to the vest. But I can't resist the curiosity in her face. Or the challenge. The bartender drops two shot glasses, a salt shaker and two limes on a napkin. "Hold out your hand," I say gruffly, salting the space between my thumb and first finger. I do the same for Sparky. Without breaking eye contact we lick the salt from our hands. My body pulls tight as I see goosebumps erupt on the exposed flesh at her neck. Electricity zips down my spine. "Ready?"

She nods, still holding my gaze and reaches for her shot, only breaking eye-contact when she tosses back the alcohol. I'm overcome with the need to taste the citrus on her tongue, to sip the bite of tequila from her lips. "Another?" she says, voice bordering on hoarse.

I shake my head. "Not yet. First I want to know why you keep pushing women on me."

She presses her lips together, even while her eyes go widely innocent. She clears her throat. "You seem… lonely." She almost gets the last word out without a laugh. *Almost.*

"Ha. Ha," I punctuate slowly. "It's gonna take a lot more than that to break me."

"We'll see," she says coyly. "But you know…. making out isn't making love. Maybe what you need is a good old-fashioned make-out session." Her mouth twitches again. "You know, to take off the edge?"

I can't deny I've had the same thought. The problem is, the only woman I'm remotely interested in making out with is the one I can't have. And the more I try to push her from my mind, the more she's all I can think about. I glance across the bar. A blues band has started up, and Owen catches my eye. He nods, then goes back to dirty dancing with a woman I don't recognize. The rest of the team is paired off and kicking it up.

Sparky follows my gaze. "You should join them."

"Not interested," I growl.

She rolls her eyes, making a noise deep in her throat. "You'd rather pout?"

My heart pounds, feeling too big for my chest. "No."

"Jesus, Steele. What is it, then? You've been as grouchy as a bear coming out of hibernation."

I turn on my heel. If I don't leave now, I'll do something I regret.

"Steele," she calls after me. "Where in the hell are you going?"

She follows me out to the parking lot, and the van we've rented for the duration.

"I'm going back to the hotel."

"But the guys-"

"Will be fine. They can Uber." I pull out the keys and reach for the door.

Sparky's hand lands on my forearm. "Steele," she says sharply. "What the fuck gives?"

Her hand is like a brand. In quick succession, the keys clatter from my hand, jangling to the asphalt as I spin us both around, caging her in against the side of the van. "You want to know what the fuck gives? I'll give it to you straight Sparky. I can't fucking sleep. I can't fucking breathe without thinking of you. And not the normal kind of thinking about you. The sexy, dirty kind of thinking about you that involves mouths and teeth and fingers and bare skin. I can't get you out of my head. And when you parade other women in front of me in an attempt to get me to break - *it fucking pisses me off.* Because I don't want to take the edge off with some willing stranger. I want to take the edge off with *you.*"

Chapter Fifteen

I think I might lose myself in Sparky's deep brown eyes, the way they widen and search my face, looking - I'm sure - for some kind of indicator that I'm bullshitting her. I grab her hand and press it against my heart. "I swear I'm not fucking with you. Can you feel this?" My throat feels tight, raw. As if I've been screaming.

"I… we…"

"Can't." I finish for her. "But that doesn't mean I don't want." I shut my eyes with a heavy sigh, anchoring myself to the tiny warm hand beneath my own. Guilt gnaws at me. "I'm sorry. I shouldn't have said anything."

She flexes her fingers into my flesh. Two pink streaks color her cheekbones and her eyelids flutter down. She whispers so softly I barely hear it. "I want, too."

I'm pretty sure my heart stops beating for a full three seconds. I feel like I'm teetering on the edge of a knife, and I don't know which direction is worse. On one side lies ruin, the other, regret. Neither is an acceptable option. I'm at a loss, because hearing those words from Sparky is the last thing I expected. But now I don't know what to do. It isn't just a question of to kiss or not to kiss. It's a question of how much risk am I willing to live with? How far into the danger zone do I want to step?

My dick pretty much answers for me. *All the fucking way.*

I slip a finger under her chin and gently pull. "Sparky," I warn. "I don't do crewmance."

"You don't do any romance," she corrects.

Her acknowledgement stings. But it's the truth. "I'd do it with you, though."

She snorts. "That's cute, Steele. The road to hell is paved with good intentions, too."

"Soo… no kiss?" I'd be an idiot not to try.

Her nostrils flare as she exhales through her nose, mouth pursed into a little rose. "Probably not."

"Not even one? Just for laughs?"

Her eyes snap to mine. "There's nothing funny about kissing you, Steele." Her voice is like a razor, sharp with pent-up desire, and the force of it hits me like a ton of bricks.

With a muffled curse, I push back from the van and turn my back. "Go back to the bar, Mariah," I say, using her given name. "Because I swear to God all I want right now is to kiss you senseless."

My insides are in turmoil. My face is hot, my hands and feet cold. All the blood has rushed to my dick, and I need a fucking moment to get my shit together.

"Steele."

The way she says my name pulls at something deep inside me. Strikes a chord of longing I'm unprepared to face at the moment. "*Go, Mariah,*" I say through clenched teeth. "Let's forget this conversation ever happened."

I wait to turn around until I'm sure she's gone. Still, a small part of me is disappointed she didn't stay.

Chapter Sixteen

FROM THE TEXTS OF MARIAH SANCHEZ AND HER SISTER

Mariah: Soooo.....
Cecilia: How'd it go?? Did you win?? big smiley-face emoji
Mariah: Of course. We set a new course record! bigger smiley-face emoji, confetti emoji
Cecilia: And you're back at the hotel already?? What kind of lame-o are you?
Mariah: A pretty big one, apparently.
Cecilia: Grrrll... go get your party on!
Mariah: I think I'm going to wash my hair and go to bed.
Cecilia: That sounds like code for something happened. Wanna talk?
Mariah: Nah. I know it's late there.
Cecilia: There's no difference between talking with my mouth and talking with my fingers. I'm awake either way.
Mariah: I almost kissed Harrison.
Cecilia: YOU ALMOST KISSED HARRISON STEELE?!?!?!?!?!

Dots appear. Dots disappear. Dots appear again.

Cecilia: AND YOU WAITED THIS LONG TO TELL ME?!?!?!?!? angry face emoji.
Mariah: Don't yell at me. It didn't happen.
Cecilia: ... But you wanted it to ...
Mariah: .... yeah :(
Cecilia: grllllll- you know you're playing with fire.
Mariah: DID I MENTION I *DIDN'T* KISS HIM?!?!? angry face emoji
Cecilia: But you wanted to, and that's just as bad. You know he's a player...
Mariah: But the way he looked at me, CiCi... I think I melted just a little.
Cecilia: He's not worthy. He will break your sweet heart.
Mariah: But I really like him. heart eye emoji
Cecilia: broken heart emoji
Cecilia: Look. You know I'm your biggest fan, and I'm not going to tell you how to live your life, but seriously, be careful, and for fuck's sake, make him work for it.

Chapter Seventeen

"You look a little rough around the edges," says Lisa, Danny's head bartender, as she pushes a drink my way. "Too much fun after hours?"

"Not nearly enough," I state dryly giving my whiskey a swirl.

"Wanna talk about it?"

"Did Danny put you up to this?" It would be like him. Danny plays a good game of tough guy, but he looks after his own.

She grins. "Maybe. But maybe my motherly instincts are kicking in." Lisa pats her bulging belly.

"Tell you what," I say after taking a hefty gulp of my beverage. "You tell me who the asshole was who knocked you up and skipped town, and I'll tell you what's on my mind."

Lisa's face pulls tight. "No deal."

She's a hard nut to crack. We've all been trying for months to find out who the jackass was that left Lisa high and dry, but she's having none of it. Danny's instructed all of us to look out for her - not that we wouldn't anyway.

The little baby is going to be overwhelmed with eight of us competing to be number one uncle.

"So…" Lisa puts a glass of water next to my whiskey. "Who are you taking to the gala, and please tell me you've found a date for Danny. He keeps trying to get me to go."

"No and no." Normally, I'd have arm candy lined up by now - the biggest philanthropic event of the year is taking place next weekend at the Nelson. Steele Conglomerate is always a sponsor, and I always make the most of free publicity. But this year, I've dragged my feet finding a date. "Maybe I'll ask Danny," I joke. Sort-of.

I think there's something seriously wrong with my dick. I've tried, truly tried, since we came back from Oregon. But every woman I've taken on a date has been a dud. Uninteresting, too self-absorbed, wrong eye-color, wrong hair, wrong laugh. And I couldn't bring myself to do anything more than give them a peck on the cheek. Worsening the situation is the fact that Sparky has called after each one of my dates to ask how it went. And that each time we've stayed up way too late talking. I leave a single hundred on the counter for Lisa. She won't let us help, so we've taken to giving her enormous tips.

As soon as I step foot into my loft, I speed-dial Sparky.

"Don't tell me you blew another date?"

"Nope, but I *do* have a proposition for you."

"Don't think you can get out of your wager than quickly."

I ignore the needle and charge ahead before I lose my nerve. "I'd like you to be my plus-one at the Gala next weekend."

"*The* Gala?"

"It's not that big of a deal."

"Are you kidding me? *Everyone* knows about the Gala."

"Well, it doesn't have to be a big deal for us. There will

be food, wine, and dancing. I'll chat up a few of the important donors, and then we can go home."

"Home? As in your home?"

"Sure." I shrug. "Why not?"

She makes throaty sound. "I'm not so sure—"

"Just as friends. I won't even hold your hand."

"But I don't have a dress."

"You'll have ten days to find one." She makes another doubtful noise. "C'mon. It'll be fun, and I promise, no talk about kissing or sex."

Her laugh crackles over the speaker. "Are you sure?"

"About the fun? Yes."

"What about… the other?"

"Scout's honor."

"Were you even a Scout?"

I grin and shake my head. "Nope, never."

"I'm not quite sure I can take your promise seriously."

"How about I swear on the boat?"

"Are you kidding me? Don't you think that's a bit sacrilegious?"

"Not if it convinces you to be my date."

"Isn't there a difference between plus-one, and date?"

"Not for me. I promise I'll be the perfect gentleman."

She waits at least ten seconds before answering softly. "What if I don't want a perfect gentleman?"

The teasing, flirty sound in her voice has my cock immediately jumping to attention. "I can be as ungentlemanly as you like." My voice drops an octave.

"I'm sure you can," she says with another little laugh.

"Please, Sparks?"

She lets out a deep sigh. "Okay, I'd love to be your date."

The tightness in my shoulders releases with her acceptance. We may not be able to kiss each other, but I'll make sure she has a great time.

"Pick you up at 6pm Friday?" I'm practically giddy.
"Don't worry, I'll take an Uber."
"Are you sure?"
"Positive."

Chapter Eighteen

FROM THE TEXTS OF MARIAH SANCHEZ AND HER SISTER

Mariah: Sis….
Cecilia: You ready for your big night?
Mariah: no… crying emoji, facepalm emoji, crying emoji
Cecilia: Why? What's wrong? … Do you need me to come over?
Mariah: What I need is a 2x4 to the head, or some serious liquid courage.
Cecilia: Why the anxiety? You look stunning in the dress you showed me.
Mariah: I don't belong there.
Cecilia: Like hell you don't. If Super Steele asked you, you belong.
Mariah: This is a pity date. I don't belong.
Cecilia: Gurrlll… you gotta get out of your own way. You're smart, you're attractive, you're a badass in the boat… and… you know more about 16th Century Spanish Literature than anyone I know.
Mariah: I also work the bar at the President. Someone's bound to recognize me.
Cecile: tongue sticking out emoji. Who cares? Just because you work a side-job at a hotel doesn't mean

you're not entitled to have fun. Go have fun with Harry and fuck the lot of them. It's none of their business what you do.
Mariah: It's not a side job, and his name isn't Harry. It's Harrison. Or Steele.
Cecile: Aww it's so cute how you defend him. Heart eyes emoji, heart eyes emoji, star eyes emoji.
Mariah: Shit it.
Mariah: Shit… I meant shut it. SHUT IT… Fucking autocorrect.
Cecilia: laughing emoji, laughing emoji, laughing emoji
Cecilia: You really like him, don't you?
Mariah: I'm trying not to. I swear.
Cecilia: broken heart emoji
Mariah: I know, I know. But he makes me laugh.
Cecilia: broken heart emoji.
Mariah: And he sent me flowers.
Cecilia: wide-eyed emoji
Cecilia: Pictures or it didn't happen.

dots… dots…

Cecilia: HOLY SHITBALLS they're enormous!!
Mariah: big smiley face emoji
Cecilia: Jesus. He must really like you.
Mariah: Harrison doesn't like me. At least not in the way you're implying.
Cecilia: I'm not so sure, hon. Maybe you should test the waters.
Mariah: But what about your worries about him breaking my heart.
Cecilia: That was before it's obvious that he likes you. Maybe you should go for it.
Mariah: and ruin the dynamic in the boat? No thank you. No crewmance. We both know this boat is my key to

getting back on the Olympic team… Besides, you're the one who's been telling me to stay away.
Cecilia: There's more to life than getting on the Olympic boat.
Mariah: I'm not hustling two jobs for shits and grins. In a few years I'll be too old. This could be my last chance.
Cecilia: All I'm saying is that if Hunky Harry turns out to be more than the shallow man-whore you've painted him to be, that you might want to give him a chance.
Mariah: Too risky
Cecilia: Please, sis. Learn from my mistakes. Otherwise you're going to turn into a spinster cat-lady like me.
Mariah: And maybe I'm okay with that.
Cecilia: Then you'd be lying.

Chapter Nineteen

I check my watch for the third time in ten minutes. She's late. It's not like Sparky to be late. *Ever.* In the three years I've known her, she's always first to arrive anywhere. A knot takes hold in my sternum. She wouldn't stand me up. *Are you so sure?* A deeper part of my conscience asks. I'm positive. But the seed of doubt has been planted. My phone buzzes, but I feel no relief when I see it's Sparky.

S: I'm soooo sorry. There's an emergency at my other job. I have to go in.

I blink. She has another job? How come I've never known this? Once again my guilty conscience stabs at me. *Because you never asked, dumbass.* I shoot off a quick reply.

H: I can pick you up after? We can grab a late bite.

I can see the dots forming and reforming. As if she's just erased her original reply.

S: That's super sweet of you, but I'll be here late. Raincheck?

My stomach sinks. I don't want a fucking raincheck. But I don't want to be an asshole either. I check my temper and quickly write back.

H: Sure. Another time.

I pause, and against my better judgment add something else.

H: Holler if you need anything.
S: heart emoji. Thanks. And thanks for the flowers, they're lovely.

At least she likes the flowers. Maybe I've overplayed my hand. But I wanted her to know how much I was looking forward to this evening. I wanted her to feel… special. I shove my phone back into my jacket pocket and scan the room. Already, I'm calculating the minimum number of minutes I need to be here. I'll work the room, flirt with the ladies, and get the fuck outta here. Maybe go for a late night run. I spy Danny across the room chatting up a very hot redhead. He's dateless too, which means he can be my wingman until we buzz out of here. By the time I'm within earshot of Danny, it's clear there's something going on with Ms. Red. I've never seen him like this - hungry, on edge. Usually he's cool as a cucumber. I clap a hand on his shoulder. "You might want to put your tongue back in your mouth, pal," I say low enough no one else can hear. "I could see the sparks flying between you two from across the room."

Danny turns. "I thought you had a date?" His implication is clear. Ms. Red is off-limits.

I scowl, half-pissed, half- embarrassed. "Ditched me."

Danny's mouth widens into an amused grin. "No fucking way. Kansas City's most eligible bachelor is flying solo at the gala of the year."

"Not solo." I wink. "You're going to be my wingman."

Danny shakes his head. "Oh, no. I told you I'm never doing that again."

He's referring to the time when we were both at Stanford and I dragged him to a frat party that didn't end well. "Aww c'mon. That was years ago. How was I supposed to know Samantha's friend was dating the president of TKE?"

"Because these are the things you bother to find out when you push your friend into the arms of a strange woman."

"Okay, I won't blow it this time. I won't push you into anyone's arms unless it's Red over there." I tilt my head in the direction of the redhead he was chatting up earlier.

"Sorry. No can do," he says. "I promised Muffy I'd tend bar until the flasks were handed out."

Muffy Templeton. Now there's a piece of work. Old Kansas City money with too much time on her hands, despite the number of charity boards she's on. "Always behind the scenes, pulling strings like a puppet-master. When are you going to let go and start enjoying life?"

Danny sidesteps my question entirely. "Where's Stockton?"

Stockton is typically my wingman when we fly solo, but all the bribery in the world couldn't convince him to join me tonight. "He refused to come because his mother keeps trying to set him up with one of Muffy's granddaughters."

Danny covers a laugh. "Stockton's mother has been trying to marry him off since college."

"It's only gotten worse," I growl. "She's taken to 'dropping by the office' with a new girl each week."

"Sounds like you could use a drink." Danny steps around me to the makeshift bar and fills a tumbler of whiskey directly from the cask. "Tom's Special Reserve," he says handing me a tumbler of amber goodness.

I raise my glass with a rueful smile. "To snatching kisses and kissing snatch. May one of us have success tonight."

Danny narrows his eyes. "Who is she?"

"No one," I answer too sharply. If Danny got wind of anything between me and Sparky, the whole boat would know within the hour. Not to mention I would be the recipient of incessant and indefinite razzing.

"Liar. Your eyebrow always twitches when you lie." He points to the corner of my eye. "Whoever she is, she's got you tied up in knots."

I make a face. "The only tying up going on will be happening later tonight." If only. I have half a mind to march over to Sparky's and wait on her porch until she gets home. Half a mind to kiss her silly and tell her all bets are off. And if tying up were part of the negotiation, I'd be game for just about anything with her.

"But not with Roxi. Just so we're clear." Danny sticks me with a look that clearly says Red is off-limits.

"Roxi, huh? That her name?" The corner of my mouth curls up. He may not know it yet, but Danny's a goner.

"Don't get any ideas. My love life's off limits."

I spread my hands, the picture of innocence. "I just want to help."

"You want to help? Spread the word — discretely — about tonight's poker game."

I jam my hands in my pocket. Maybe a poker game is just what I need to blow off the steam building inside me. Danny's games are big. You either win big or lose big. And I'm not in a mood to lose tonight. "What's the buy in?"

"Fifty." He means thousand. "Limited to the first five. If we have ten, I'll do a second seating at one."

I nod. A night of poker and whiskey will put Sparky far from my mind. "See you at midnight?"

Chapter Twenty

I've got a few hours to kill before heading to the Whiskey Den. I'm out of sorts, and still bugged that Sparky stood me up. I leave the Nelson, and head downtown. I have half a mind to hit the office for a few hours, but I'm too restless, there's too much energy in my body and no place to put it. If I wasn't locked into a stupid bet I'm determined to win, I'd hit the nearest nightclub and take some willing thing back to my place.

But I'm not fucking doing that, goddammit.

Instead, I decide to go vintage and hit the President Hotel. They have a cigar room, and there will be jazz. I can lurk in a corner drinking whiskey and brooding to my heart's content. I don't go there often, only with a certain type of client I'm trying to woo. But it suits my mood perfectly. I toss the keys to the valet and walk through the doors that I swear are original. Across the plush carpet to the elevator that zips me up to the top floor and a spectacular view of the Kansas City skyline.

The hostess greets me with an overly enthusiastic smile and leads me to a table in the corner. It's pretty empty, but for a piano player on the dias, a cocktail waitress who's currently helping a couple of older guys in suits, *and Sparky behind the bar.*

I do a double-take, not believing what I'm seeing, but it's definitely her, wearing a black tee and black pants. "Some emergency," I mutter. I rise, and make my way to the bar, sliding into a seat right in the middle. "And here I thought you were off saving humanity, a lá Don Quixote."

She gasps and turns, eyes wide. "What are you doing here?" She narrows her eyes.

I raise my hands and speak before she does. "I swear I'm not stalking you. Just a crazy coincidence. I didn't know you had a second job until you ditched me."

"Can I get you something?"

"Jameson, neat." She doesn't deny she ditched me. I look around the room. "Looks super busy," I say, mouth twitching. "Yep, total emergency."

She tosses a rag into the sink. "A colleague needed help."

I sniff. "I smell eau de chicken shit."

Her mouth twitches, and two pink spots stripe her cheekbones. "I smell *I can't take no for an answer.*"

"I took no just fine. It's the excuse I'm not buying. C'mon, admit it. You chickened out." She starts drying glasses and putting them away. "Let me guess. Someone needed a shift covered and you jumped at the opportunity." The color on her cheeks deepens. "Am I right? Because it was either that or stay home translating Cervantes, and you were too chicken to text me that you'd rather stay home reading old Spanish tomes than go on a date with me."

She raises her eyes to mine. "Okay, you're half right. I chickened out."

"So you admit you would have rather stayed home?"

"No. I was dressed and ready to go."

My voice softens. "So what happened, Sparks?"

"I chickened out. Big fancy parties aren't my thing." She pulls the Jameson from the shelf and pours it into a glass.

"They're not mine either."

"But you're used to them. They're part of your world. People like me work big fancy parties. We don't attend them." She pushes my drink across the counter.

I drop my hand on top of hers, before she can pull it away. I get what she's saying, and it never occurred to me that she'd feel that way. "I'm sorry I made you feel uncomfortable."

"I'm sorry I didn't level with you. You deserve better."

"I'm sorry I pushed too hard."

She snorts. "What is this, an apology-fest now?"

"I'm entirely certain I can outdo you with apologies."

"I'm damn sure you can't."

"We can thumb wrestle do decide the winner."

Her mouth twitches at the corner. "You're a dork."

"I'm pretty sure the dork prize belongs to you Ms. *I want a PhD in Sixteenth Century Spanish Literature,"* I tease.

She flashes me a grin. "Just remember, I can curse at you in both ancient and modern Spanish. Skillz."

I stare at her over my whiskey, and can't help but wonder what other *skillz* she's kept under wraps. I sure as hell am going to enjoy finding out.

Chapter Twenty-One

FROM THE PERSPECTIVE OF STEELE'S DICK

If chasing pussy were an Olympic sport, I'd win all the gold. I know how to leverage my assets, use my charm and my good looks. Women eat me up like pints of Ben & Jerry's. Except I'm so much better than B&J. I live as much for the chase as I do for the outcome. There's nothing quite like the exhilaration of the chase. It's better than booze, or high stake poker, or Christmas Morning. And the gratification that comes when the chase is successful? Epic - for both me *and* my partner. E.P.I.C. Because I make it goddamned unforgettable.

But none of my tricks work with a certain tiny lady with balls of steel. Not one. And I'm beginning to worry she might break me. Because it's been ***six*** months.

SIX

What the fuck is he thinking? I'm losing my goddamned mojo. And when we finally get some action, I'm going to shoot off like a fucking thirteen-year old, thereby embarrassing both of us.

Chapter Twenty-Two

New Year's Eve

I sense Sparky's presence before I see her. I turn, scanning the room, and find her making her way to the bar. I grab two champagne flutes and head to intercept her. "You look amazing," I say, dropping a kiss to her cheek and handing her a flute. Amazing is perhaps an understatement. Her dress floats around her the way Marilyn Monroe's did over the subway vent. But Sparky's dress is a brilliant shade of turquoise blue - the kind of blue that makes you think of beaches and snorkeling… and skinny dipping.

"Thank you," she murmurs, pink staining her cheeks. "And thank you for inviting me."

It was totally spur of the moment, inviting the team to the Steele Conglomerate annual New Year's Eve bash, but we're losing our number two stroke Trevor, to a job in Boston, and this is our last hurrah. "The whole team's here. It wouldn't be right to ring in the new year without you."

I usher her past the packed dance floor and over to a high top where the team's hanging out. The guys let out a series of low whistles when they see Sparky. "Damn, Sparks, you clean up good," gushes Owen.

"Promise you'll save me a dance?" adds Mac.

Hot green poison pools in my belly, but I force myself to let it go. They're just looking after her, which is what I should be doing too, if I wasn't tied up in knots. She looks around the group, then back at me. "Where's Danny?" Leave it to Sparky to not miss a thing. Danny's been an honorary teammate of sorts, ever since we started.

"He's been laying low since everything blew up at the Whiskey Den."

Sparky gives a sympathetic nod. "It sucks when you lose everything."

She speaks like she's been there, and I want to get her to a quiet place and find out why. Even after nine months of regular nightly phone calls, she's played her cards close to the vest. Offering up only glimpses of her private life. But I've been no better. I haven't shared anything deeply personal either. Maybe that changes tonight.

She brightens. "Have you guys thought about asking him to replace Trevor?"

"We've asked him before," Stockton says with a shake of his head. "Answer's always the same."

"Maybe it'll be different this time," she suggests. "You know, New Year, New You?"

"I like it," says Mac. "We could all make New Year New You resolutions."

"I hate resolutions," I growl, draining my champagne. "Terrible idea."

"Oh?" Sparky answers with a grin. "Too far outside of your comfort zone?"

"I think they're great for goal-setting," says Jackson.

"Sure, if you need that kind of thing," I agree. "But I set goals all the time. I don't need New Year's Eve to do it."

Stockton eyes me. "I think it's too personal for you."

He's not wrong. Already, I can feel the discomfort brewing in my gut. If I have a goal, and I'm not saying I do, it would be to end this crazy chemistry between me and Sparky once and for all. Scratch the itch and move on. She's had my cock in irons for nine months, sixteen days, twelve hours, and… I check my watch… forty-seven minutes. That shit ends tonight. But the team will eat me alive if I confess it. I change the subject. "I don't need a resolution, because I'm happy with my life."

Stockton chortles. "You've been celibate for nine, almost ten months, and you're happy about it?"

Mac perks up. "What's this? Harrison Casanova Steele has been celibate? How'd I miss this?"

Beside me, Sparky's shoulders are shaking, and she looks very interested in her empty glass.

"When was the last time you've seen him with an arm draped around a boat bunny? presses Stockton. "I want to know what kind of deep zen enlightenment you've achieved by keeping your dick under wraps."

"Wait, did you say *nine months?"* asks Owen. "For real?"

A quiet giggle escapes from Sparky's mouth.

"So *that's* why we had the best season ever," Jackson adds. "You've had a bad case of blue balls."

"I wondered why our speed was phenomenal this season," says Owen. "Maybe I should give up sex too."

"*No,"* I say too sharply. "That's a dumb idea. I only did it because… because I bet I could. But that deal's off." I swing my gaze to Sparky who quickly looks away. "No more one-night stands. I'm holding out for the real-deal."

Mac sweeps a hand across the room. "Good luck with that. I bet any single woman, and a lot of the married ones would happily help you discover *the real deal*," he ends with a snicker. "Take your pick."

Sparky comes to my rescue. "Guys. You didn't win because Steele kept his dick tucked in. You won because you're an amazing team. And if you want to win again this year, we're going to have to up our game. Starting first thing tomorrow. We've got less than twelve weeks for the Thames race again, and you know the local boys will be gunning for us. They're pissed as hell that a bunch of cocky Yankee bastards stole their title."

"Earned it," Jackson growls.

"Of course you earned it, but they'll always think it was rightfully theirs." She gives all of us her *don't fuck with me* stare. "You need an experienced rower to jump into Trevor's seat. More importantly, you need someone you can trust. Danny seems like the obvious choice."

Stockton looks my way. "We could sweeten the pot. Now might be the time to tell him about our idea for the distillery out at the baseball field."

I look at Jackson, Mac, and Owen. "How do you guys feel about offering Danny a spot in the owners box?"

"Sure, why not?" answers Mac.

Owen nods his agreement.

"I'll head downstairs and write something up. See you all at the gym first thing?"

"Seven-thirty," Sparky affirms amidst the groaning protests of the guys. "New Year, New Team," she says with a grin. "Trevor, why don't you ask me to dance? We can leave these guys to cry in their whiskey about tomorrow morning."

"Sure thing," Trevor answers with a grin.

I resist the urge to go all caveman as Trevor ushers Sparky out to the dance floor. I make up my mind right then and there, that I'll be kissing Sparky at the stroke of midnight. Come hell or high water.

Chapter Twenty-Three

It's nearly eleven-thirty. Sparky has taken rounds on the dance floor with everyone but me. Her eyes shine with excitement, and something tugs deep inside me. She looks almost… happy. Maybe it's the champagne, or the plans being made for the next season, whatever it is, it radiates from her like sunshine sparkling on the lake. She catches my eye and grins as she floats by in the arms of one of my upper management guys. Evan's a good guy. The kind of nice guy you bring home to your mother, but I'm having none of it. No sirree. I put down my drink, and make a beeline for the dance floor. I'm in position the next time they circle round, and I tap Evan's shoulder. "May I?"

He looks chagrined when he sees it's me. "I can't exactly say no to the boss, can I?"

"Not this time."

"Thank you Evan. It was nice to meet you," Sparky says with a smile that would give any dude a boner.

"The pleasure's all mine. See you around, Mariah?"

Heat coils in my stomach. The way he says her name makes my blood curdle.

She nods, slipping into my arms just as the music slows,

and the singer begins to croon the opening lines of *At Last.* My hand lands at the small of her back, and I pull her close. "You've been having fun this evening."

She tilts her head up. "I haven't had this much fun since… I don't know when."

"Good. I think you work too hard."

"Cute, coming from the man who thinks four hours is a good night's sleep."

"Work hard, play hard," I quip.

"Indeed." Her eyelashes flutter down.

There's so much I want to say to her, and I don't know where to begin. I settle for the feel of her pressed against me, for the way her tiny hand is encased in my own. At the high point of the song, she glances up, face unguarded for once. My mouth goes dry from the wanting, the longing. "Mariah." My voice comes out choked.

"Yes?" I hear breathless anticipation in her voice, so much emotion. As if she's been longing, too.

"I still want to kiss you," I murmur, voice dropping to the basement.

She bites down on her lower lip before glancing away. Her cheeks flush dark pink, and I swear I can feel her nipples puckering against my chest. She nods. "I think we need to talk."

"I'm not interested in talk right now."

"I'm not either, but we need to."

That… wasn't the answer I was expecting. Hope surges through me, and I lead us to the far corner of the dance floor, away from the prying eyes of my teammates. "Come upstairs with me?"

She nods and lets me lead her to the service exit. We slip down the deserted hallway that will take us to the main bank of elevators, our echoing footsteps the only sound between us. I punch the main elevator button, still holding onto her hand like it's a fucking lifeline. My heart thumps loudly in my ears. We step into the car, and the door shuts behind us with a whoosh. If I were less of a gentleman, I'd kiss her senseless right here. But I want to hear her out. And honestly, what's a few more moments of torture?

She sucks in a breath as the doors open to my office suite. It takes up half the top floor. Thick plush carpet spreads in every direction. We skirt the receptionist's area, and the boardroom, and head back to my office, which overlooks Power and Light. "You live here too?" She asks with surprise in her voice, as she catches sight of the bedroom off my office.

I grin. "Only when I'm working on a deal. Sometimes it's just easier to catch a few winks here, and then start the day again."

"You totally work too hard, then."

I shrug, "It's paid off. And the rest of my C-team has beds in their offices too."

"So *all* of you work too hard."

"No time for sleep when you're building an empire."

She turns to me. "And what comes next? After you've built it?'

Her line of questioning makes me uneasy. "I guess I've always thought I'd know when the time was."

"Hhmm," she grunts, surveying the space again.

"Nightcap?" I offer, moving to the sideboard.

"Sure." She kicks off her shoes and follows me to the liquor cabinet.

"What's your poison?"

She clears her throat, and I swear she muttered *you* under her breath. "I'll have what you're having."

"How about this?" I pull out a bottle of 2015 Côte Rotie. "I've been saving this for a special occasion."

"Sounds perfect," she says lightly, settling herself on the big leather couch that takes up one wall of my office.

I join her and hand her a glass. "New year, new you." We clink glasses and take a sip.

"Mmm, delicious." Her eyes shut as she savors the flavor. I watch, rapt, as she swallows. She is the very embodiment of sensuality.

"I surrender," I say hoarsely, unable to take it any longer. "You made your point, bet's off."

Her eyes fly open. "Why? What changed?"

Everything. Can't she see that? "What changed, *Mariah*, is that I'm uninterested in anyone but you. I go to sleep thinking about you, you interrupt my thoughts during the day. I wake up with your name on my tongue. Every time something good happens, you're the first person I think of telling. I want to kiss you, I want to get down and dirty with you, I want to know what you look like when you climax, and for fuck's sake — I want to know how in the hell you got that scar over your left eyebrow."

She stares at me for a full second, before bursting into laughter. Not exactly the response I was hoping for. My stomach sinks. But in true Sparky fashion, she does the unexpected. She takes my glass and places it on the coffee table next to hers, then climbs into my lap and begins to loosen my tie. "I got the scar when my older sister, Cecilia — CiCi— threw a Barbie doll at me." She pulls my tie off and folds it neatly, setting it aside before attacking the top button of my shirt.

"Mariah." My voice is full of gravel. "What are you doing?"

"What does it look like I'm doing?" she teases with a flirty smile.

My cock is hard beneath her, hotter than a three-alarm fire. "Are you sure?"

"Mmm, most definitely," she says with a nod.

"But I thought you wanted to talk."

Her hands stop moving. "Do you really want to talk?"

"No, but—"

"Then shut up and kiss me," she says lowering her head.

She doesn't need to ask twice. If there's one thing I know I'm good at, it's seizing opportunity. This opportunity may never come again, and I'm sure as hell not going to miss it. Her lips are soft against mine, sweetly sensuous, and so *so* much more amazing than I'd imagined. Her kiss sets off a raging inferno inside me, like a spark to gasoline. My thighs tense, every neuron in my body fires. With a groan, I wrap my arms around her and take over the kiss. I flick my tongue across her lower lip, and her mouth opens with a sigh, tongue meeting mine stroke for stroke. She tastes like wine and sunshine, and the promise of unending bliss. I'm hungry for so much more of her, but it's been so long since I've kissed anyone, I'm content to make out on my couch as long as she likes.

Chapter Twenty-Four

FROM THE PERSPECTIVE OF STEELE'S DICK

Can I just say *that it's about DAMN TIME?!?!?* Jesus fucktits. Can I also say that you can tell so much about a woman by the way she kisses? Sparky is no exception. There's a latent sensuality packed into her kiss, soft and languid like a hot summer day. She's a slow burn, this one. And she's not afraid to ask for what she wants. Which I like, because I fucking aim to please. And by god, I intend to rock her world so hard, she never wants anyone else.

Chapter Twenty-Five

I'm not sure how long we stay there, lip locked. We're both breathless when we part, and I dimly register the sounds of fireworks outside the building. "Happy New Year," I rumble thickly.

"Happy New Year," she mumbles back, mouth still pressed against mine. She kisses me again, hot and sweet, and it's better than any high I've ever experienced. My eyes about roll into my head when I rock my erection against her, and she grinds back.

"God, Mariah," I say when we part again. "What do you want from me?" I half expect her to climb off me and walk away, now that we've kissed. While it's not my first choice, I'd understand why.

"I want my one night," she says breathlessly, dropping her mouth to the hollow at my neck and gently biting. Lust rips through me, and god help me, I want her to bite again.

"Are you drunk?"

She bites again, and my cock jerks beneath her. I know she feels it, because she rocks against me, harder this time. "Nope. Definitely not drunk."

"Why? Why now?"

She braces a hand against my shoulder and pushes herself away. Her eyes are dark pools, glazed with raw heat. "Because I've had a crush on you since forever, and this year I'm doing things differently."

My head snaps back, and I can't help the grin that spreads across my face. How did I miss this? I mean, I could tell she wanted me after I told her I wanted to kiss her, but before? How could I have been so blind?

Easy, when you're chasing pussy, asshole, my conscience chides.

"You're sure about this?"

She leans in and takes my mouth in a slow, hot kiss, tongue sliding against mine. I can barely breathe from the exquisiteness of it. "I'm very sure," she murmurs once she pulls back. "I've wanted this, *you* for a very long time."

Her confession socks me in the gut. I'm not worthy of her deep affection. I haven't done anything to deserve it. Yet it's there. And suddenly, the stakes feel a whole lot higher than a one-night-stand. This is Sparky — my confidante, my teammate, and fellow ass kicker. I want to give her everything she's fantasized about and then some. "I don't want to break you," I blurt.

"You won't. But I might break you."

Her words bring sweet relief, because I know for a fact, I can't be broken. I thread my hands through her hair, and nip at her lower lip. "I promise I'll make this good." God, I'd give her anything she asked for right now.

She gives me a lopsided grin. "I'm banking on it, hot stuff." Her mouth lands on mine while her hands fiddle with the rest of the buttons on my shirt. Her touch is as confident as her mouth, and I can't help the groan that escapes when her fingernails scrape across my chest. I flex my fingers into her scalp, loving the feel of her silky dark hair sliding through my hands. I could fucking kiss her mouth all night long. I draw a hand down the column of her neck, down the exposed skin of her back, and back up to the clasp of her halter. I make short work of it, and the front of her dress falls away.

I suck in a harsh breath. Her tits are more perfect than I remember, high round globes with dark nipples, erect, and waiting to be pleasured. "You're fucking perfect, Sparky," I say on a ragged breath. I brush my thumb across her nipple, delighting in the way it puckers and goosebumps rise across her skin. She moans, arching her back, when I take it in my mouth, lapping and swirling my tongue over the hard peak. I do the same to the other, going back and forth until she's writhing in my lap, breath coming in short gasps.

I lift my head and our eyes lock. She flashes me the most wickedly delighted grin. If I wasn't a goner before, I am now because, holy hell, it's hot as fuck. My cock is like iron, but he's just gonna have to wait a little longer. I wrap my arms tight around her and rise. Her legs hook around my hips, and I stride to the bedroom, place her gently on the edge of the bed, and drop to my knees. She gives me a look of hungry anticipation, and opens her knees with a flick of her eyebrows. The scent of her arousal fills my nostrils. It's heady as fuck, better than any high. My hands tremble ever so slightly as I push up the soft material of her dress, exposing her thighs. "Lean back," I say, voice full of gravel. She drops back to her elbows, eyes fixed on me.

So she's a watcher. I like that. For some reason that turns me on even more. It also strengthens my resolve to give her one mind-blowing orgasm after another. I slide the palm of my hand up her thigh. Her skin is as soft as silk. Anticipation rises within me. Are her curls going to be as wild and untamed as the last time I caught a glimpse? Or has she done something entirely different? My other hand takes the same path, and I press against her inner thighs, thumbs caressing the crease where legs meet torso. She lets out a tiny sigh. I glance up with a grin. "Yes?"

She nods, answering with a grin of her own.

I reach farther, brushing the fabric that separates me from paradise. "You're soaked," I murmur, glancing up again.

"Take them off," she says, lifting her hips.

I'm only too happy to oblige. I hook my fingers through the sides and tug. I can't help but chuckle when I catch a glimpse of them. I was expecting something racy and lacy. Instead, they're pink polka dot cotton briefs.

"Don't judge," she reprimands with a sheepish grimace.

"Oh, I'm judging," I tease.

"Do you have lacy special occasion briefs?"

I scoff. "Of course not."

"Right? Totally impractical."

I never thought of it that way, but I see her point. "I love how practical you are."

"For real?"

I nod. "You're unlike anyone I've ever met, Sparks."

The air grows heavy between us. Serious, even. My chest grows tight as we take each other in. This is as honest and raw as I've ever been with a woman. It's simultaneously terrifying and exhilarating. I caress her legs again, just to ground myself. This is a one-night-stand. Nothing more. And I'm going to make it the best night either of us have ever had. I bend, and plant a kiss inside her thigh, letting her scent wash over me, pushing the fabric out of the way as I make my way closer to her pussy. When I reach her apex, I pause, checking in with her again. She's right there with me, watching avidly, mouth parted. I have to kiss her. How can I not kiss that perfectly plump mouth? I rise, clasping a hand behind her neck, and kiss her. Soft little brushes at first, until she leans in, opening her mouth to receive me. She kisses with abandon, with the same fierce energy she uses to drive the boat, letting me lead, but only so far, because she's too used to calling the shots.

"More," she breathes, when we part. "I want more."

"Patience, grasshopper," I say, mouth curling up. "I'll give you everything you want and then some." I drop to my knees again, pushing her skirt out of the way so I can take in her pussy. It's damned near perfection. Dark pink folds, glistening with arousal peek through a tangle of dark, damp curls. She's an untamed garden. Wild and free — just like her personality. I fucking love it. I hesitate, heart in my throat, the weight of this moment pressing on me— but only for a moment. Then I dip my head and kiss the tender skin next to her folds, letting my breath warm her skin, before moving over to the place I've been fantasizing about for far too long. I breathe her in, the sharp, clean, scent of her arousal. I blow over her sensitized skin, and a shiver ripples through her.

"Stop teasing," she pants. "Please."

I oblige. I press my tongue into her slick folds, searching, lapping, slowly making my way toward her engorged clit. Her sighs fall on my ears like water, and her hand comes to my head. I take my time, learning each dip and rise, feasting on her arousal. Her hips begin to rock as she offers up her most secret parts, seeking more friction. I seal my mouth around her clit, licking with the flat of my tongue. She pulls on my hair, grinding against my mouth. She's close, too close. I'm amazed at how fast she got there. I pull away only to have my hair yanked. "Don't stop," she grits. "Don't you dare stop."

I chuckle, and place an open kiss on the inside of her thigh. "I promise the wait will be worth it."

"Tease," she growls.

"Maybe just a little." I kiss the inside of her other thigh, and draw the back of my finger across her swollen folds. I kiss her hipbone, the soft swell of her belly, I stroke her legs in long fluid motions. Only when her breathing slows, do I dive back in again, kissing the center of her, devouring every inch until she's at fever pitch again. She curses when I pull away again. A beautiful string of profanity that's music to my ears. This time, when I make my way back to her pussy, I pause. "Look at me Mariah." Her head rises and our gazes collide. She's like a woman possessed, wildfire in her eyes, hair tousled from writhing, cheeks flushed, lips swollen. "I've never seen you look so beautiful," I say, barely able to speak. The feeling inside my chest is too big, too much. If it were anyone else but Sparky, I'd run for the exit. But I have to see this through. Hell, I want to.

Keeping my eyes on her, I settle myself between her legs. The sweet bright taste of her is like a homecoming of sorts. Something deep inside settles into place. I lick and lap, suck and swirl, while I watch her, rapt. Her orgasm is a thing of beauty, the way it transforms her face. She lets out a loud keening cry as shudder after shudder wracks her body. I keep my mouth on her until she's spent.

"Holy shit, Steele," she says with a giggle. "What the fuck was that?"

"Only the first round."

Chapter Twenty-Six

"How many rounds are we going?" she asks, eyes sparkling.

"As many as you want, sweetheart." A cloud crosses Sparky's face. "Did I say something wrong?"

She props herself on her elbows. "I'm not your sweetheart."

"I know," I say, keeping my voice light, hating that she's pointing out the obvious. "Slip of the tongue."

"I can't be your sweetheart," she presses.

"I know. And don't worry, our little tryst will remain a secret forever, if that's what you want."

"I want."

I hate the wave of disappointment that makes my stomach sink like a stone. But she's right, we have to put the health of the boat above all else. I crawl up the bed, and settle next to her, propping my head on my hand. "What else do you want?" I waggle my eyebrows, setting off a cascade of giggles.

"How many condoms do you have?"

"Enough for us to go all night long if you like."

"I shouldn't spend the night. We've got training first thing."

"And Stockton and I want to pay a visit to Danny before that."

Her face turns concerned. "Do you think he'll join?"

"We're not going to take no for an answer."

"Danny can be pretty stubborn."

"We're making him an offer he won't refuse."

"Oh?"

"We're going to set up a distillery at the ballpark, and offer him a spot in the owners box."

Sparky lets out a low whistle. "That's very generous of you."

"It's the right thing to do."

She cocks her head, eyes soft. "You're a good man, Harrison."

I warm at the way my name rolls off her tongue. "And you, *Mariah,* are damned near irresistible."

She blushes the sweetest shade of rose. Sweeter still is the way she tilts her chin to receive my kiss. A tremor pulses through me. I don't deserve this kind of trust. Not from her. I haven't earned it. Not in this way, at least. She trusts me because of the boat. The way we all trust each other. But this is different territory, scarier territory. At her request, this is supposed to be platonic. Nothing more than a wild night between two consenting adults. But it's not. It's so *so* much more than that. Feelings I don't want to acknowledge balloon in my chest. I push them aside and deepen the kiss, letting my mind run wild with the myriad of dirty activities before us.

"So tell me," I say with gravel in my throat, when we part. "What are your limits?"

Her eyes widen. "For real?"

I nod.

"Wow. No one's ever asked me that before."

I growl in disgust. "They should have."

She tilts her head, studying me. "Noted."

"Well?"

Her eyes light, and she taps a finger against her lower lip. "Hmmm… Okay… anal play okay, anal sex, not."

"Spanking?"

"Light, but I'll tell you if I want more."

My cock strains against my slacks, desperately wanting to be set free. "What else?"

"I'd let you tie me up… with your tie. But only my hands."

"Positions?"

She shoots me a naughty grin. "We can get as bendy as you like." I grin back. But then she surprises the heck out of me. "What are *your* limits?"

I blink. No woman has ever asked what my limits are. Not once. I like it. And my mind goes to a very dirty place. "I have none."

"You must have some."

"Nope."

"Toys up the ass?"

"Bring it."

She giggles uncontrollably. "Tying up?"

"Yep."

"*Spanking?*" Her eyes are wide as saucers, and sparkling with laughter.

"Come to daddy."

She snorts. "Are you kidding me?"

I shake my head.

"You've done all that stuff before?"

"Nope. But I would with you." The weight of my confession only hits me after the words leave my mouth. The balloon in my chest returns. And expands when she cups my cheek.

"Why?" she asks quietly.

"Because I trust you. And I really like you, Sparks. And I feel like we have this connection."

"I feel it too."

"And even though this can't go anywhere. We can just be in the moment, and enjoy it. And each other."

She nods. "I know what you mean."

I swallow, words stuck in the back of my throat. "Do you ever—"

She stops my mouth with a finger. "Shhh. More kissing, less talking."

I agree, but at the same time, I want her to know that if it was any other time or place… I'd want it to be different. Something… more.

Sparky pulls on my neck, bringing my mouth to hers, and while we kiss, her hands are everywhere— pushing off my shirt, tugging at my belt, and oh, jeezus, cupping my balls. "I meant it when I said your junk is perfect," she murmurs between kisses, as she draws her hand along my rigid shaft, squeezing right beneath the crown. My eyes roll back. It's been so fucking long since I've been touched, I've forgotten how good it is. And her fingernails. Motherfucker it's going to take all my self-control to hold out.

"God, you're amazing," I mutter from somewhere deep in my throat. She responds with a giggle and a bite to my collarbone.

Somehow, our clothes end up on the floor, and we're stretched out on the bed, skin to skin. The sweet spicy scent of her fills the air, and for an awful moment my heart squeezes so hard it hurts to breathe. I don't want tonight to end. I don't want it to be what I've always said I wanted— one night only. God help me, I want more. I reach for a condom, and her hand covers mine. "Let me."

She tears it open, but before she puts it on, she drops her head, and runs her tongue along the flared edge, before taking the head into her mouth. My body goes hot and cold, every cell firing to life. "Jeezus, Sparky," I grunt, unable to say anything more. Words have left my brain. I'm functioning on a purely primal level.

"Next time," she murmurs as she rolls the condom down my shaft, ending her ministrations with a gentle tug on my balls.

With a caveman-like growl, I flip her onto her back, and press her knees apart, settling my hips between her legs, cock notched at the entrance of her very slick pussy. I take her hands and pull them above her head, capturing them both in one of mine. I tease at her opening, sliding through her folds, until she expresses her impatience with another string of curses. I slide into her, slowly. Inch by inch until I'm fully seated, surrounded by her tight heat. And jesus, she's tight. Her pussy grips me like a vice. I pause, memorizing the feeling. I don't ever want to forget this moment, the sensation of being completely enveloped.

She starts to move first, slow little rocks as she searches for the angle she likes. I hold still, thrusting only when she starts to take on a rhythm. She lets out a guttural moan that spurs me on. "Yes, deep like that. And slow."

I hold my pace, even as electricity races up my legs, and draws my balls tight. I'm a fucking rower, I could take this pace all night and let her come all over me as many times as she wants. I'm barely winded, but my own orgasm winds up, and hovers at the edge of my awareness, ready to launch when I let go. I give her exactly what she wants, driving deep and hard, keeping up the slow pace that set her body on fire. And when her back arches off the bed and in an earth shattering orgasm, I'm right there too, tumbling over the edge with her into the great abyss.

Chapter Twenty-Seven

FROM THE PERSPECTIVE OF STEELE'S DICK

Oh sweet baby jeezus. I think I need a cigarette. Or a joint. Maybe four.

That is all.

Chapter Twenty-Eight

By four a.m. we've gone through an entire strip of condoms. I'm spent, and want nothing more than to spoon for a few hours before Sparky makes me haul my ass to New Year's Day training. "You should be grateful I'm giving you an extra hour," she chides, gently socking my shoulder.

"Just a few more minutes?"

She lets out a husky laugh. "I never took you for a cuddler, Steele."

I'm not. But this is different. And I'm not ready for it to end. But she's made it clear our time's up. I push to sitting and reach for my pants. I hand over her dress. "I'm keeping your panties."

"Perv."

"Maybe."

"Totally."

"I'll wash them and keep them in a drawer. You know… in case you come over again."

A look of pure regret washes over her face. "You know there won't be a next time," she says gently. "There can't be."

I give her a lopsided smile. "A guy can hope, can't he?"

The ride back to her place is quiet. She lives in one of those vintage buildings on Armour. "Can I walk you to the door?" I shouldn't be worried about her safety, Sparky can fend for herself. But I can't help it.

She turns in her seat. "That's very sweet of you, but I'll be okay." She sucks in a breath. "Harrison?"

My stomach yo-yos. "Yeah?"

"Thank you for this. I'll never forget it." She leans across the console and presses a kiss to the corner of my mouth.

The most exquisite pain blooms across my chest, and for a second, I can't speak. "Me either," I finally manage to croak.

"Are we good? Back to business as usual?"

I nod. "We're good. Hands off from here on out."

She flashes me a brilliant smile. "Good. See you at seven-thirty. Don't be late."

Chapter Twenty-Nine

FROM THE TEXTS OF MARIAH SANCHEZ AND HER SISTER

Mariah: HAPPY NEW YEAR confetti emoji, confetti emoji, confetti emoji, sent with fireworks.
Cecilia: … Why are you up?
Mariah: I never went to bed :D
Cecilia: OH? Did you ring in the new year with some hottie?
Mariah: you could say that… giddy emoji
Cecilia: WHO?!?!?!? SPILL
Mariah: I'll give you three guesses… crazy emoji
Cecilia: You didn't.
Mariah: Maybe… laughing emoji
Cecilia: OMG YOU DID!!!!! DID YOU?!?!?!
Mariah: I did.
Cecilia: fireworks emoji, confetti emoji, confetti emoji, crazy face emoji
Cecilia: And?????????
Mariah: I don't kiss and tell.
Cecilia: I'm your sister. I don't count.
Mariah: Let's just call it the best night I've ever had in my life. Ever. And I'm super sad it's over.
Cecilia: Why is it over?

Mariah: Too risky.
Cecilia: For you? or the boat?
Mariah: … both
Cecilia: oh hun.
Mariah: It's okay. I knew what I was getting into. Itch Scratched.
Cecilia: Still…
Mariah: I think I'll be okay. I have to be okay.
Cecilia: You know where the B&J pints are. Come on over. We can have ice cream for New Year's breakfast.
Mariah: Can't. Practice at 7:30. They're bringing in fresh meat. crazy face emoji, laughing emoji
Cecilia: You're evil.
Mariah: It's part of my charm.

Chapter Thirty

Sparky's waiting for us at 7:30, looking far too fresh-faced given our night. She practically glows. "You guys look a little worse for wear," she says with a decidedly evil grin. "Time to sweat those toxins out of your bodies." She swings her gaze to Danny, who we've convinced to join the team. "Welcome to hell week, Danny. If you work hard, you'll catch these softies in no time."

"Who's calling who softy?" Challenges Mac, flexing his pecs.

Sparky laughs maniacally. "Lace up your shoes, we're going for a three-mile sprint, followed by a thousand on the erg."

The erg - a rowing machine to those not in the know. Otherwise considered an instrument of torture to rowers. We barely keep up with her. Danny straggles, and Stockton is right there with him. Twenty minutes in, and they're both heaving into buckets. I'd be heaving too, if I had any food in my stomach.

"Sip your water, don't gulp," she cautions. "Hop on the erg as soon as you can."

"Happy fucking New Year," Owen mutters under his breath.

"Happy fucking New Year to you too," answers Sparky as she practically dances by, a broad grin on her face. "This is the year we PR every race. This is the year we go undefeated. This is the year we put Kansas City on the map. Am I right?"

We all mutter some form of agreement. But it's not good enough for Sparky.

"*AM I RIGHT?!?!*"

We all answer at the same time, with a little more conviction.

"Yes."

"Hell, yes."

"Fuck, yeah."

"That's more like it," she says, snapping her towel. "Onto squats."

She brutalizes us for the next hour, but we can't complain, because she's running, and lifting, and pushing right along with us. It's why we'll do anything for her. She's not some queen bee perching on the cox box. She's one of us. She's our motivation and in many ways, the heart of this boat.

By the time we wrap, we're sweaty and exhausted. Danny cracks a smile for the first time since the Whiskey Den got raided. "I needed this. Thanks."

"Don't thank me yet," Sparky says with a low chuckle. "You'll be cursing me out before the end of the week."

She's not wrong. But she takes it in stride. And we all know without a doubt, we'll be the leanest, meanest boat on the water come March.

~

It's nine-thirty, and I'm pacing my loft like a caged lion.

I've talked to Sparky nearly every day and not calling her feels weird. Wrong. And If we're going about business as usual then I absofuckinglutely should call her. Or at least text her. I've spent most of the day with the guys drinking beer and watching bowl games. We all agreed our training diet starts tomorrow. And after the workout Sparky threw at us this morning, we deserved all the beer carbs our bodies would allow.

I pull out my phone, thumb hovering over the digital keyboard. "Fuck it," I mutter. I hit the call button.

She picks up on the second ring. "Are you drunk dialing?"

"No," I scoff.

"But you *have* been drinking?"

"I had beers with the guys earlier."

She tsks. "A moment on the lips…"

"Training diet starts tomorrow."

"Fair enough. I cheated today, too."

"What'd you do?"

"Had New Year's lunch with the fam in Prairie."

"You need a new car if you're going to drive out there." Prairie, Kansas is a good three hours from Kansas City. It's where our baseball team hosts an exhibition fundraiser with a bunch of veterans. It's a typical small western town, with one light and a diner with the best pie I've ever had. But Sparky's car is a piece of shit. And the thought of her breaking down in the middle of the Flint Hills with no cell service, turns my insides cold.

"Sure, with that twenty-grand of pocket change I have in the couch cushions," she says sarcastically. "I'll keep that in mind."

"At least take my car the next time you go. Please? We can't afford to lose you." I want to say a whole helluva lot more than that, but given our agreement, it wouldn't be right. "Are you home now?"

"Yep. Sitting in front of the fire in my fuzzy pajamas drinking wine and eating ice-cream. How 'bout you?"

"Wearing a hole in my hardwoods."

"Why's that?"

All the things I want to say, but can't, because fuck-all, I want to be a gentleman. I shrug, even though she can't see it. And then I think, fuck-it. Why not be brutally honest? She can take it. "Because I really want to see you again."

"You'll see me tomorrow," she quips.

"That's not what I mean."

"I know."

My stomach knots. I should have kept my fucking mouth shut. But then she shocks the hell out of me.

"I want to see you again, too." She says it so quietly, I think I've misheard her.

"But that's not business as usual."

"I know. But it seems… it seems I'm addicted to your orgasms," she confesses in a rush.

I puff up like a silverback gorilla. I want to run around and thump my chest, roaring. I try and keep my voice steady, cool. "Is that so?"

"I have half a mind to drive to wherever you live, right now. In my pajamas. And I'm showing excellent restraint."

"By drinking wine and eating ice-cream," I supply.

"Exactly."

"Do you want company?"

"Are you offering?"

It's on the tip of my tongue to play coy, say maybe. But something shakes loose inside me. "Yes. I am," I answer boldly, heart speeding up. She could turn me down. She *should* turn me down, and remind me of our agreement. I should stay away.

"Bring your pajamas."

"I don't own pajamas."

"Then you'll have to eat ice-cream and drink wine in your boxer briefs. Are you up for that?"

"Game. On."

She opens the door clad in fleece bottoms covered in snowflakes and a tank top. Before I'm halfway inside, she's grabbed my shirt and pulled me in for a kiss. She tastes like chocolate and wine— a heady combination. I pick her up and pin her to the wall, hands skimming the flesh beneath her tank top. She yanks at the henley I'm wearing, and somehow I manage to pull it off with one hand.

"Condoms. Bedroom. *Now,*" she urges between kisses, wrapping her legs around my hips.

I'm ramped up and ready to go. "Which way?"

She flails a hand in the general direction of the living room, and by the time we collapse onto her bed, we're naked as the day we were born. She tosses me a condom, leaning back on her elbows, watching avidly as I roll it over my straining erection. I loom over her, and run a hand up the inside of her thigh, brushing my fingers over her slick entrance. It blows my mind how ready she is. I slide into her and damn if it doesn't feel like coming home. Something settles deep inside me. She must feel it too, because she lets out a deep sigh. But then she grabs my ass, digging her fingernails into my flesh. It sends a shot of lust pinballing through me. I rock into her, thrusting hard, then slowly pulling back. "More," she says with a dark grin. "Yes."

I'm only too happy to oblige, because the sensation is enough to bring me right to the brink. Beneath me, she's panting, clawing, meeting me thrust for thrust, bearing down and encasing my cock in a vice-like grip. "I'm close, Mariah."

"Me too," she gasps. "Oh, me too."

I feel the second she starts. Her legs go tight, and she moans long and low, her pussy rippling against my cock. I can't hold back another second, and I let go with a loud grunt, emptying myself into her, pushing into her softness with everything I have. My vision spots and I collapse to my elbows. "Holy shit, Sparky."

She giggles, eyes dancing. "Thank you for that."

"So much for business as usual," I say with a shake of my head.

Chapter Thirty-One

Business as usual, my ass. Business as usual becomes sneaking around like delinquent teenagers. And I fucking love every second of it. Except for the part where we're keeping this from our teammates. Sparky's just as hard on me in practice as she's always been. And I'm impressed with her ability to compartmentalize. The first week in March, we put the shell in the water for the first time. It's a cold, rainy morning, and we're bundled up. But the regatta on the Thames where we'll return to defend our title, is less than 4 weeks away, and although Danny has fully integrated into the team's psyche, it's going to take a few weeks of rowing with him to sync the rhythm in the boat.

A stiff wind blows out of the north, and Fitz wants us rowing right into it. Confusion reigns. Sparky's calling strokes from the stern, while Fitz travels along in a boat shouting instructions through a megaphone. It's annoying as fuck, and one of the worst practices we've had in ages. Everyone's grumpy and soaked when we pull out. My hands ache with fresh blisters, and every muscle in my body's on fire.

"That was the sorriest bit of rowing I've seen from you lot in ages," shouts Fitz. "And *you.*" He turns to Sparky. "What kind of training operation have you been running?"

"Same as usual, sir," answers Sparky with a determined expression.

"They're flabby and slow. We've got four weeks to look like a team, not a bunch of hacks. And if you can't get them rowing together, then maybe we need to shake up the boat."

"Now hold on a sec," I start, but Fitz cuts me off with a wave of his hand.

"You guys had a stellar season last year. But if you can't sustain it in the off-season, then you're not the team I thought you were." He stalks off grumbling.

I've always known Fitz had a temper, but I've rarely seen it. I want to punch him for humiliating Sparky that way. I glance her direction. Her face is stony, jaw set, pulse throbbing at her temple. "Fuck that asshole," she says once Fitz is out of earshot. "I have not poured my blood sweat and tears into you to have Fitz break up this boat. What the fuck happened out there?" She eyes each of us.

Danny raises his hand. "I'm still slow. My stroke was choppy. Especially at the catch."

"How are you going to fix it?"

"I think I've gotta dig with my legs more."

"Then do that. Anyone else?" She stares us down.

Mac raises his hand. "I was thinking more about Danny's stroke then my own."

"Stop that," she says with a tight smile. "What's the best way to get in sync?"

"Match your stroke the to the guy in front of you," volunteers Owen.

"Can you all spare another hour? I'd like to get back out there and run slow drills. We need to bring Danny up to speed. There's a new vibe in the boat, and we just need to settle in."

I've never been more proud of her. "I can stay." Which means most the team will stay since they work with me.

"Me too," says Danny.

"Alright, let's put her back in the water."

For the next hour, Sparky takes us through beginning drills. Stuff that high school boats practice, but it works. At the end of the hour, we're at least rowing in unison. We still have a long way to go before the boat swings, but I'm confident she'll get us there. I hang around after the guys depart, under the guise of helping put stuff away. "You okay?" I ask, grabbing a rag and helping Sparky dry the shell. "You know Fitz is an asshole."

She nods.

"I thought you were great out there today. And by the end we didn't suck."

She huffs out a breath through her nose and nods again.

"Sparks?"

"I'm fine," she says thickly.

She's not. I drop the rag and close the distance between us, pulling her tight against my chest. "I'd have punched him if he kept going," I promise.

Her shoulders shake. "No you wouldn't. You'd ruin the boat if you lost control like that."

"But he'd deserve it."

"Yeah. But still, it's not worth it. It was just a tough day today."

She stays snug in my arms for who knows how long. Long enough that I start thinking dangerous thoughts. "I want to tell the team."

She stiffens. "I think that's a terrible idea."

"I don't think they'll mind. In fact, I'm pretty sure Stockton already suspects."

"Oh no, are you serious?" She steps out of my embrace, and I feel the loss of her.

I nod. "He's too discreet to say anything, but I have a hunch."

"We need to stop, then," she says firmly.

"Do you want to?"

She stares up at me, jaw still set firmly. "No. I don't. But this boat means everything to me."

My gut clenches. "What about me? What do I mean to you?" I shouldn't ask that. I don't have the right. We're just having fun. So much fun I've started to fall for her.

"I really like you, Harrison. You know that."

"But?" My stomach drops. I don't want there to be a 'but'. I want her devotion.

She sucks in a breath like she's going to say something, then thinks better of it. "I really like you. Can we leave it at that?"

"Have dinner with me tonight," I press. "Let me take you out on a proper date. Bring you flowers. You can wear that dress you wore at New Year's."

"What if we're seen?"

"So what if we are? There's no rule saying we can't date." She still looks unsure. "I'm tired of hiding, Mariah. And quite frankly, you deserve better. *We* deserve better." Her eyes widen at my use of her given name. But I'm tired of fucking around. "I want everyone to know I care about you."

"What about the consequences? What about the fallout if this runs its course?"

"Damn the consequences. We're adults. If it runs its course, it runs its course and we part as friends."

"Would we?"

"Why not?" I narrow my eyes. "I'm not an asshole. I'd never dream of cheating on you. We both love the boat. We both respect each other, I don't see that changing."

"You don't have a crystal ball."

"Neither do you." I cross my arms, determined not to give an inch. "Give us a chance, Mariah." This is as close as I've ever come to begging.

She worries at her lower lip, teeth clamping down on it. My heart pounds so hard, I swear I can hear it. I'm not used to being held at arm's length. Until Mariah, I've always been the pursued. Now the tables are turned and it's deeply unsettling. "A compromise?" She asks after an ice-age has passed.

"Anything."

"I'll go to dinner with you. We can hold hands, kiss in public, whatever you like. But I don't want to tell the team."

I scowl. "Why not?"

She rolls her eyes. "Because I'm the only woman, for starters. I have no desire to be slut-shamed because I'm dating someone in the boat."

"I swear to god, I will beat—"

"That's just it, though. Don't you see? I don't want to have to rely on you, or anyone else, to defend my honor. And inevitably, it will come to that."

I hate to admit it, but I see her point. "Fair enough. So do we have a deal?"

The corners of her mouth curl up, and relief washes over me.

"For now," she says.

Chapter Thirty-Two

FROM THE TEXTS OF MARIAH SANCHEZ AND HER SISTER

Mariah: I'm out. We're out.
Cecilia: it's about damn time.
Mariah: thanks for that.
Cecilia: Well, it's true. I don't like that you two have been sneaking around like you're some big naughty secret. It's not healthy.
Mariah: Well, if you must know, he was the one insisting we come out.
Cecilia: I like him more and more.
Cecilia: … have you told him?
Mariah: told him what?
Cecilia: That you're being recruited?
Mariah: No.
Cecilia: Don't you think he deserves to know?
Mariah: When it's a real thing and not a fantasy.
Cecilia: Do you honestly believe you're not going to get a spot?
Mariah: bird in thc hand, sis. bird in the hand.
Cecilia: What else haven't you told him?
Mariah: nothing.
Cecilia: Sis…

Mariah: grimace emoji
Cecilia: You need to tell him you're being recruited.
Mariah: Not until I've secured a spot. It's too up in the air. And I don't want to rock the boat.
Cecilia: Ha. Ha.
Mariah: I mean it. I think I'm in love with him. And I can't be if I'm going away.
Cecilia: Maybe you should try talking to him?
Mariah: as soon as I know something. I promise.
Cecilia: facepalm emoji, facepalm emoji, This is going to bite you in the ass. You know that don't you?

Chapter Thirty-Three

FROM THE PERSPECTIVE OF STEELE'S DICK

So what if I'm pussy whipped? Mariah Sanchez has pretty much ruined me for anyone else, and you know what? I'm damn okay with that.

end. of. story.

Chapter Thirty-Four

"You look ravishing," I say, heat spreading across my chest as Sparky opens the door. She's wearing *that* dress again. The one that takes me right back to New Year's Eve.

"Are you sure? I feel like I've worn this a lot lately," she says, accepting my kiss.

"Hell, yes. I don't understand why you women can't wear the same dress more than once. Besides," I say, dropping my hand to the small of her back as I escort her down the hall to the rickety elevator in her building. "This dress always makes me think of our first time together." My hand drops lower, once we're ensconced in the tiny space. "And taking it off."

"Perv," she says with a little giggle, firmly placing my hand on her hip.

"Guilty," I admit, dropping a kiss at the hollow of her neck. The elevator jerks to a stop, and I wrestle with the gate. It takes a full minute before we're able to exit. "Have you ever thought of moving out?"

"No way. It's one of the most affordable condos in the

city. I don't want to move out to the 'burbs. Too white bread."

"You could move in with me," I offer. "Working elevator, convenient location."

She stops in the middle of the sidewalk, brows knit together. "That's why I should move in with you? Because it's *convenient*?"

I can instantly see I've bungled my ask. The question is, how do I un-mess it up? "You wouldn't have to work your second job," I say. "You could start back to school if you wanted."

"So I should move in with you *so you could take care of me?*" Her expressions darkens. "I appreciate the offer, but not only can I take care of myself, but it's plenty convenient to stay where I am, thank you." She turns and marches down the sidewalk to the car. I swear I can see steam coming out of her ears. "I'm not a charity case."

My own hackles rise. "I never said you were."

"Not all of us were born with a silver spoon, and every advantage. There's no shame in hustling."

"Of course there's not. Shit, I've hustled with the best of them."

"But you haven't had to hustle to survive," she points out.

"True, but the work ethic is the same. You do a good job of hiding it, but I see how tired you are. I see how hard you work, the exhaustion around your eyes when you work a double. And dammit, Mariah, I'm in love with you. Why wouldn't I want to help make your life a little easier? There's no shame in that either— wanting you to not have to struggle so hard. Wanting to help you achieve your dreams."

I didn't plan for this conversation at all. And that's my problem— I should have. I should have wined and dined her, seduced her, and then asked her to move in. It's come out all wrong, and now we're nearly yelling on the sidewalk in front of her apartment building, late for a fundraiser. I rake a hand through my hair. "Look, Sparky— *Mariah.* I meant what I said. I'm crazy about you. I love you. I want to be with you. And dammit, I want to give you an easier life. Let me take care of you."

Her face turns bright pink. "I don't need to be rescued," she says, staring at the cement.

I close the distance between us and drop my hands to her shoulders. "Look at me Mariah." At first, she stubbornly keeps her eyes averted. I soften my voice. "Please? Please look at me?"

My heart melts when I see the tortured look in her eyes. "I don't want to rescue you, Mariah. I don't have some kind of a savior complex I need to satisfy. I want you to move in because I love you. I want to be with you, spend more time with you, not less. And yes, if that means you don't have to work so hard, that's great too."

"But my family—" she starts, then hesitates.

"What about them? Do you think they won't approve?"

"Oh I know they won't approve. But they didn't approve of my useless major in college either. Or the fact that I've pursued rowing and not teaching."

"But this is different," I acknowledge. "Don't you want your family's approval?"

"About the person I love, too?" she offers quietly. "Yes."

My insides grow warm at her admission. I'd hoped. I'd even resigned myself to not having those feelings returned. But now that she's said it, I want to shout it from the rooftops. I kiss her forehead. "We can talk about this more later, but the offer stands."

She nods, and lets me help her into the car. It's a quick drive over to the fundraiser taking place in the ballroom at the top of the President. The owners of the local sports clubs get together every year to raise money for community sports leagues across the metro. I'm representing the rowing club tonight. Stockton will be here representing the Kansas City Kings. It's a pretty informal event. We all show up with our checkbooks and our dates. A couple of the kids' coaches give speeches. We drink cocktails, we go home. The closer we get to the hotel, the more agitated Sparky becomes.

"What is it, sweetheart?"

"Just a little nervous, that's all."

I slide a hand up her thigh as I pull into valet parking. "Nothing to be nervous about. Just be you. Talk about how rowing changed your life. These guys love a good story."

The guy running valet recognizes Sparky. "Hey Mariah, didn't expect to see you here tonight. Slummin' it, huh?" he says with a laugh as he takes my keys.

She laughs with him, but the laugh never makes it to her eyes. Instead, she shoots me a worried glance. She blanches when the elevator opens on the top floor and the first person we see is Stockton. "Don't worry," I growl, as I lock eyes with my business partner, then notice Penny, his genius hacker assistant on his arm. "Stockton's not going to breathe a word to the team."

"Why is that?"

Stockton glances at Mariah, then scowls at me. I tilt my head toward Penny, and raise an eyebrow. For half a second, we glower at each other, then reach a silent agreement. I take Sparky by the elbow and lead her directly to where Stockton and Penny are standing. "Stockton, Penny," I say.

"Sparky," acknowledges Stockton. "This is Penny, my… ah…"

"Colleague," I supply.

Sparky extends her hand. "So nice to meet you. I row with these guys."

Penny nods and opens her mouth to speak but is cut

off by the booming voice of Big Jim Williams, owner of the pro-football team. "Well if it ain't my two favorite rivals," he booms. "And who are these pretty ladies you gents have brought along?" His fleshy lips pull into a lascivious grin. My blood curdles. Slimy Jim is more like it. How he didn't get caught up in the human trafficking bust that took place last fall is beyond me. I'm sure the guy is dirty. I wrap a possessive arm around Sparky. Stockton does the same.

"Nice to see you Jim." There's no warmth in my voice.

"I thought you two'd be down at Spring Training."

"It's Owen's turn, this year," answers Stockton. "And with Penny here, running predictive analytics, there's no need for all of us to be in Arizona."

Big Jim shakes his head. "All that technology. Don't make up for what your eyes tell you. And speaking of eyes," he turns his gaze to Sparky. "You're a cute young thing. You should come dance with my girls. We could use some flavor like you to spice up the dancers, if you catch my drift." His eyes rake over her figure.

Sparky stiffens, jaw set. My hand curls into a fist as red flashes at the sides of my vision. What I wouldn't give to break this asshole's nose. But as big as I am, Big Jim is my height and twice as wide. Regardless, if we weren't at a fundraiser, I'd fucking take my shot. "I already have a job," Sparky says stiffly.

"Still," Jim persists, leaning in and breathing like a freight train. "Girls like you can do well."

"And what exactly is a girl like me?" she asks sharply.

Pride for her swells inside me. I fucking love her grit.

"Well, ah… you know," he huffs. "We got lots of fans who like those Spanish señoritas," he says.

Sparky goes in for the kill. "How very nice. But you see, I'm not a girl. And my ancestors have been here, *in America* since the fifteen-hundreds. Furthermore, you couldn't pay me all the money in the world to join an organization like yours. Your team culture embodies the worst of the sports industry, and with all due respect, culture starts at the top."

Penny sucks in a breath. I glance over at Stockton who looks like he's biting the inside of his cheek to keep from laughing. Big Jim sputters, face growing mottled. He glowers at Sparky, then swings his gaze to us. "You—"

Stockton beats me to it. "Might be time to rethink your business model, Jim."

I step closer, and lower my voice so only he can hear. "You ever talk to my girlfriend like that again, I will be waiting for you in a dark alley. Do we have an understanding?"

Jim glares, opens his mouth, then snaps it shut. I can only imagine the vitriol spewing in his head right now. Just so long as it doesn't come out of his mouth. I turn back to Sparky. "Let's grab a drink at the bar." She's visibly shaken, and it kills me. I signal the bartender. "Two Jameson, neat."

"Drink," I say, handing her a tumbler. "Jim's a first-rate asshole. I'm really sorry."

"Welcome to my world."

"What do you mean?"

"I mean just that. No one's ever, not in a million years, going to treat you the way I was just treated." She downs her whiskey in one long gulp, slamming the glass on the counter. "Do you know what it's like to have people look at you with suspicion? Like you don't belong? Follow you through a drug store when you're shopping for toothpaste?" She grabs my drink and downs it, too. "And you know what's the worst? Is that the richer people are, the more insidious their barbs. They pretend to be all enlightened, but really, they're just as racist as the poor guy down the street."

"Hon, I'm so sorry. Not everyone's an asshole like Jim."

She swings a tortured gaze my direction. "How do you know? I don't want to walk on eggshells bracing for the next awkward encounter from some donor you have to be nice to."

"You won't have to, Mariah. Look at our organization. Has anyone ever even given you the side-eye? Treated you with less than utter respect?"

She shakes her head. "But how can you understand what it's like? People automatically respect you."

"I can't. You're right, I've never walked in your shoes, but I can sure as hell make sure that shit doesn't happen again."

She gives me a sad smile and shakes her head. "You can't. You can't be there to protect me all the time. And I don't want you to." She looks like she wants to say more, lots more. "I'm… gonna go home."

"Mariah—"

She places a finger across my lips. "Let me go, Harrison."

Panic races through me. It feels like she's slipping away. "Don't go, please."

She stands on tiptoe, placing a kiss on my jaw. "I'll see you 'round."

And because I don't want to make a scene, I let her walk away.

Fucking hell.

Chapter Thirty-Five

I dread practice the next morning. By the time I've reached the reservoir, I've already sweated through my base layer. Sparky is the first one there, as usual, and except for the way she avoids my gaze, it's business as usual. In fact, we have our best split yet. In the boat, she's the consummate pro. Meeting my eyes dead on, and calling the strokes. We work seamlessly together, and it's weird, because my chest has never ached so profoundly.

After we stash the shell, Fitz gathers us around. "You've come a long way. Especially you, Danny. I think we're going to be in great shape for the season opener."

Sparky clears her throat. "I have something I'd like to say." The way she looks at me sends ice through my veins. "This is the best boat I've ever been a part of, and Fitz is right, I think you're going to kill it in London."

I glance over to Stockton. She didn't say *we.*

Her voice catches. "And I want you to remember that, because I'm not going to be with you."

Everyone starts talking at once.

"Hold up," she shouts over us. "It's not because I don't want to. I'll be there rooting for you, from the National

Team selection camp. I have a shot at a spot on the Olympic boat." Her eyes sparkle with excitement.

I'm the first to yell, and I sweep her up in an embrace swinging her around. The rest of the guys join me in their congratulations. It's great news, what she's always wanted. I kiss her on the cheek. "I'm so happy for you, Sparks." I mean it too. I want her to chase this. I swallow back the selfish disappointment, because this is it. Our fling has run its course, and even though I've fallen hook, line, and sinker, it's not meant to be. It feels like the disbanding of the Fellowship of the Ring. "When did you find out?" I ask once the accolades have died down.

She flashes me a guilty glance. "Two days ago." And she didn't tell me. My stomach sinks to my toes. And her decision to go was made so much easier thanks to last night. She lays a hand on my arm. "I wanted to tell you."

"But you didn't," I answer tonelessly.

"I'd planned to tell you last night, but—"

"Big Jim happened," I fill in.

She nods, eyes full of sympathy.

"I don't want your sympathy, Sparks. I thought I meant more to you than that," I snap, not caring that I've just outed us to the whole team.

"You do. You mean everything to me. You know that."

"Do I? Then why not trust me enough to tell me?"

"Because for a hot second, I thought I might not take the spot," she snaps back.

"Well that's dumb. Of course you'd take the spot."

"And maybe I needed to work that out for myself before I told anyone," she shouts. "Like I said, I don't need a fucking fixer."

"I thought I was your partner," I yell back. "For chrissakes, Sparky. I'm in love with you. What more do you want? Just because I want you to be safe doesn't mean I want to control you."

"And just because I said I loved you too doesn't mean I want to be treated like a china doll."

I'm so pissed I could throttle her. Or kiss her. Definitely kiss her. She's sexy as fuck when she's riled up. But there won't be kissing and making up this time, because my teammates look like they want to make mincemeat of me.

"What the fuck is this?" Owen asks, waving a hand between the two of us.

"Yeah." Mac crosses his arms. "What the fuck?"

I step forward. "We fell in love, okay?" I glower at my teammates. "Anyone has a problem with that, they can see me in private."

Chapter Thirty-Six

I'm three drinks deep at our new watering hole in the West Bottoms. Stockton claps me on the back. "Well, I'd say you've made a royal mess of things."

"Tell me something I don't know," I grumble. "I keep playing everything over in my head, and I can't figure out what happened."

"You're used to being in charge. So is she."

"You *are* a sonofabitch for tapping our cox. She was always off-limits," Owen reminds me.

"Yeah, but you could see the wheels turning last year in London," adds Stockton. "Something happened between you two over there."

I shrug. I won't ever spill how drunk Sparky was, or that she made a pass at me, or anything about our wager. Some things are best kept private. Even amongst bros.

"I guess it was inevitable, all that staring into each other's eyes," Owen chortles.

I give Owen the finger.

"I guess the question is," Stockton starts. "What are you going to do about it now?"

"Let her go. I'm not going to be *that guy*."

"But you also don't have to be *that asshole* either," Stockton adds. "You can let her go without being a dick."

"I don't know," says Owen. "I think he's done a pretty good job of dicking it up."

"If she gets a spot, she'll be gone for good."

"But it's not like you can't do long distance," points out Stockton. "If you wanted. We travel all the fucking time."

True. "But I think there's more at play than just the Olympic spot." I look over to Stockton. "You saw what happened last night at the sports fundraiser."

Stockton glowers. "Jim is a douchebag who should probably be thrown in jail."

"Still. Sparky was super clear about how different our worlds are."

He shrugs. "Are you going to let that stop you? You've never let it stop you before."

Also true.

Owen clears his throat. "Far be it from me to give you advice, because I'm flying solo forever, but when you look back in five years, what are you going to regret?"

Stockton nods his agreement. "I've never heard you tell any woman you love her. If you really love her, then go figure this out."

"Sparky," I call softly, rapping on her door. "Answer the door?" I rap again.

The door opens a crack. "Have you been drinking?"

"I Ubered."

"How'd you get in?"

I spread my hands. "Got lucky. Can I come in?"

The door opens a little wider, but she still blocks it.

"I promise, no funny business. Unless you want," I add.

She snorts and rolls her eyes. But she opens the door

and lets me pass. She follows me into the living room and perches at the far end of the couch. She looks so tiny and vulnerable, not the strong fierce woman I've grown to love. "I'm sorry. I behaved badly today."

She surprises me by nodding. "I am, too. I was an asshole. I should have told you. I was afraid."

"I think you getting a shot is the greatest thing ever, Sparks. And I'd never let you not go," I add, thinking back to our conversation. "We could do the long distance thing… if you wanted."

"We kind of do it anyways, with your travel schedule," she admits. "But I need my independence. I'm not ready to move in with you."

It stings, but I accept it with a nod. "The offer stands, whenever you're ready."

"Does the team hate us?"

"Surprisingly, no."

A look of pure relief crosses her face.

"Mariah, come here." I pat the space next to me. She does one better and crawls into my lap. "I'm all in. Wherever the chips fall. I'm your guy, and I'll always have your back. And if you'll let me, I'll even beat assholes like Big Jim to a pulp."

She makes a face and a noise of disgust. "Don't waste your energy. He's not worth it. But don't be surprised if that kind of shit happens again. Not everyone is as nice as the guys in the boat."

"I get it. And I won't fight your battles for you, but maybe you'll let me fight next to you?"

She sighs, and lays her head on my chest. "I'd like that."

"You know what else I'd like?" I say, because I'm only a little buzzed, and I'm still a dirty dog perv. And hell, I have a gorgeous woman in my lap.

"I can feel it," she says dryly, even as she wriggles against my quickly growing erection.

I scoop her up and head for the bedroom. "Feel like a little make-up sex?"

Her hands loop around my neck. "I thought you'd never ask."

Chapter Thirty-Seven

FROM THE TEXTS OF MARIAH SANCHEZ AND HER SISTER

Cecilia: GOOD LUCK!!!! fingers crossed emoji, fingers crossed emoji, confetti emoji.
Cecilia: We're rooting for you.
Mariah: Thx!!
Cecilia: How are you feeling?
Mariah: The good kind of nervous. The gals in the boat are great. Really synced up.
Cecilia: Harry and the guys are with me.
Mariah: THE WHOLE TEAM?!?!?!
Cecilia: Surprise! Big smiley face emoji.
Cecilia: It was Harry's idea.
Mariah: His name is Harrison. Just call him Steele.
Cecilia: Hey babe, it's me- Super Steele ;) Your sis can call me Harry. But she's the only one.
Mariah: She let you steal her phone? She doesn't even let me steal her phone.
Cecilia: I'm that fantastic. :D
Mariah: Glad to see your ego hasn't taken a hit ;)
Cecilia: Seriously babe, you're going to crush it out there today. Love you.

Mariah: Thx. And thanks for bringing the team. I have a little tear in my eye.
Mariah: Love you too! xoxo
Cecilia: So does that mean you'll move in with me?
Mariah: Nope ;) Can I talk to my sis again?
Cecilia: Sure thing. I'll be yelling loudest for you xo
Cecilia: Me again :D You should move in with him.
Mariah: When I'm ready. I've got to go. 30 minutes until our heat.
Cecilia: See you soon! Love you.
Mariah: You too, CiCi <3

Chapter Thirty-Eight

Sparky loses, by less than a foot, but her boat was tapped to be the first boat for Women's National Team. So while Olympic gold is out of reach… for now, Sparky's traveling around the country kicking ass.

As for our boat? It's not the same without her. We have a new cox, Samantha Winters. And she's great, but she's no Sparky. Our wins are sporadic. I keep asking Sparky to move in with me - especially now that she's traveling so much, and she stays here most nights when she's in town. But for all my charm, she still says no — even though there's a twinkle in her eye. I swear she's saying no just to yank my chain. But I'm a patient man, and when she's ready, I know she'll say yes — to moving in and so much more.

Chapter Thirty-Nine

Two years later

I light the candles on the table and double check the bubbly in the ice-bucket. I hear the door click in the entryway. She still doesn't live here, but at least she now has a key. That only took a year. I'm hopeful that when I ask again tonight, for the millionth time, she'll say yes. Finally.

I glance up, and momentarily forget to breathe. She's wearing my favorite dress— the turquoise one from New Year's Eve two years ago— the night everything changed. My mouth curls up, and I round the table to take her into my arms. "You look ravishing."

"Thank you. You look downright edible, yourself." She wraps her hand around my waist, fingers giving my ass a little squeeze before settling at my hip.

"You feeling like dessert first tonight?" I tease, but only sort-of. As far as I'm concerned, she's my main course, and I'll start feasting as soon as she lets me.

"Mmm, I like that idea, but I think we should have champagne, *then* dessert."

"What are we celebrating?"

"In addition to the obvious?"

The obvious being that she's officially retired from the National team, and she's starting her PhD this fall. Already the living rooms of both our places are filled with old manuscripts, treatises and tomes.

"There's more?" Anticipation curls in my stomach.

She nods her head solemnly. "If you're ready…" her voice takes on a coy lilt.

My heart thunks a little heavier against my chest. "Oh I'm more than ready, baby."

"Then would you like to have me as your roommate? Permanently?" Her mouth widens into the most adorable grin.

"No."

"No?" Her smile falters.

"No. I'd like to have you as my wife." I slip my hand into my pants pocket and pull out a ring that belonged to her grandmother Maria.

She gasps, eyes going wide. "Where'd you get that?"

"Well, with the help of your sister, I took a little business trip to Prairie." I drop to a knee. "Mariah Sanchez, you crazy unpredictable woman, will you spend every day of the rest of your life with me? Be my wife? My cox on a box? The steerer of our shell?"

With a squeal, she tackles me, bringing us both to the floor. I nearly lose the ring. "Yes, yes, yes," she practically shouts, slowing her bouncing long enough to let me put the ring on her finger. Then she covers my mouth in a kiss that quickly turns four-alarm fire hot. "Can we start practicing for the honeymoon right now?" She murmurs, smiling against my mouth and rocking her hips against my rapidly rising erection.

I roll us over so that she's pinned beneath me, and my hand has ample space to slide up her thigh. "Stroke oar reporting for practice."

My phone buzzes at the table. I ignore it, placing teasing kisses along Sparky's mouth. It buzzes again. I nip at the hollow of her neck. My phone fucking buzzes a third time. Mariah giggles. "You gonna get that?"

"Fuck, no," I growl, grazing my thumb along the swell of her breast. "Everything I need is right here."

My phone buzzes a fourth time, and vibrates off the table, clattering to the floor. "Don't move," I order, and I crawl to where my phone is buzzing a fifth time. I'm tempted to hurl it across the room until I see it's Stockton calling. My stomach clenches. It's never good when Stockton calls repeatedly like that. It usually means we've been cyber-attacked. "This better be good," I bark.

"Congratulate me?"

"What, for saving the company from the dark web? That's your fucking job." I'm pissed as hell and have a raging hard-on. All I want is to get back on the floor with Sparky.

"Ah, no. I thought you'd want to know before you read about it in the society column tomorrow."

"What the hell is this about?" I don't read the society column, and neither does he. "Is this code for something?"

"Negative. I'm engaged."

I blink. "What? To who?" I didn't even know he was dating.

"To Penny."

THE BEGINNING OF HAPPILY EVER AFTER

One more epilogue from Steele's dick…

. . .

Cox jokes aside. I still love pussy. And I'm still as pervy as a twelve-year-old boy. You might think you can tame the wild beast, but you can't. Marriage just makes us a little more respectable on the outside. I'm still going to be chasing after Sparky when I'm seventy. Turned out she was right about all that wooing and romance and shit. And I'm totally okay with that, too.

Super end. Of . Story.

~

Thank you for reading Steele and Sparky's story. If you enjoyed them, I know you're going to love Stockton and Penny. Read on for a quick peek at **O Magnet!**

O Magnet

Some women call me a prince, others call me a perv. They *all* call me a giant in the bedroom and king of their pleasure. I like it that way. As the CTO of Steele Conglomerate, and one of Kansas City's most eligible bachelors, I have no desire to settle down and become 'a man about the house.'

My mother has other ideas.

For the last six years, she's been trying to marry me off — parading all manner of heiresses, debutantes and socialites in front of me like plumed birds. All so that she can do the important work of becoming a grandmother. She's even started dropping by my office with prospects — *on a daily basis*.

But I'm going to beat her at her own game. Not only am I going to convince her I'm getting married, I'm going to pick the last woman my mother would ever choose for me… my crazy assistant, Penelope Fischer — Penny.

This is going to be so great…

A fake engagement, Pygmalian romp through the tech world featuring epic pranks, dirty sex, and a very happy ending.

Do you love sneak peeks, book recommendations, and freebie notices? Sign up for my newsletter at www.tessalayne.com/newsletter!!

Find me on Facebook! Come on over to my house- join my ladies only Facebook group - Tessa's House. And hang on to your hat- we might get a little rowdy in there ;)

Tessa's Bad Boys

The bad boys are coming to town. Grab your fan and a cool drink because things really heat up between Austin and Macey in **MR.PINK.**

She was only supposed to be a one-night stand...

You know why banned books are bestsellers? Because everyone wants what they can't have. And I want Macey McCaslin. I want her sassy mouth driving me wild, and her luscious curves under my hands. In a barn, in a bed, on a table. Whenever. Wherever.

But Macey's off-limits. So far off-limits, my brother Jason might kill me if he found out about us. He thinks I'm nothing more than a skirt-chasing manwhore not worthy to lick the dirt off her sexy little feet. And I'm definitely that, but ask me if I care? Because one taste of Macey was all it took to make me an addict. This may cost me everything, but I'm not staying away.

Download MR.PINK today

Also by Tessa Layne

PRAIRIE HEAT

PRAIRIE PASSION

PRAIRIE DESIRE

PRAIRIE STORM

PRAIRIE FIRE

PRAIRIE DEVIL

PRAIRIE FEVER

PRAIRIE REDEMPTION

PRAIRIE BLISS

A HERO'S HONOR

A HERO'S HEART

A HERO'S HAVEN

A HERO'S HOME

MR. PINK

MR. WHITE

MR. RED

MR. WHISKEY

CPSIA information can be obtained
at www.ICGtesting.com
Printed in the USA
FFHW021209081019
55435721-61214FF